To Love and Friendship

Regrets

All you need to realize one's true value

HEMA CHHETRI

INDIA • SINGAPORE • MALAYSIA

ISBN 979-8-88883-622-4

DEDICATION

"Vaastav main jahan prem hota hain
Waha moh nahi hota
Prem ka janm karuna se hota hain
Moh ka janm ahankar se hota hain."

"In the reality where there is love
There is no desire
Love is born out of humility
Whereas desire is born out of pride."

Lord Krishna never married Radha, but they were inseparable. The Lord had to travel to Mathura to kill Kansa and serve the purpose of his birth. Later, he became the king of Mathura. Radha was married to Abhimanyu while Krishna married Rukmini, Satyabhama, Jambavati, Kalindi, Mitravinda, Nagnajiti, Bhadra, and Lakshmana. What they had between them was not the ordinary bonding between a man and a woman; she was a keen devotee of him. After many years, when she was old and free from her domestic duties, she joined the palace as a maid, with the Lord's permission, just to catch a glimpse of him every day. Though she was physically present near him, she realized their separation was increasing her pain, so she decided to leave the palace unnoticed. Krishna followed her and his touch brought her to consciousness. Both knew their last moment together had arrived. Realizing that, Krishna wanted to give something to Radha. As she was very fond of his flute, he played it for her, and she merged with the Lord again.

The Lord had dedicated his flute to her; so, after she died, he broke the flute and never played it again. They loved each other so much that they were united spiritually, and there was no need for marriage.

"Love is not bound by an agreement; it blossoms when liberated. It is above earthly pleasures, rules, and laws."

She was the internal potency of Lord Krishna. She was revered as the epitome of selfless love and service toward him. "Love is a more pure and selfless emotion than being physical." They expressed the highest devotion of love by not marrying each other. The love between them was 'Parakiya', which is considered the highest form of love. 'Parakiya' means to love, not by marriage but by friendship. The name 'Radha' represents 'prosperity', and if we remove the 'R' from 'Radhakrishna', it becomes an incomplete 'Krishna'. In other words, they are one entity. They are incomplete without each other.

Krishna was leaving for Mathura to kill Demon Kansa, his uncle. Radha suddenly appeared on his way to discharge him properly. The Lord seemed most delighted, as if his journey wouldn't have been accomplished without her. One of the disciples and friends of Kansa, who was in the same chariot in the Lord's company, asked before he could further step down as to who she is. The Lord smiled, faced her, and wisely replied that people come to him, but he goes to her.

CONTENTS

ACKNOWLEDGEMENTS

Because I owe my parents, teachers, and this earth for passing bountiful knowledge; I would firstly like to thank them, whose debts, they say, all human beings need to pay before they die.

Secondly, to the Lords Brahma, Vishnu, and Mahesh who are the creator, nurturer, and destroyer.

Lastly, I want to thank the rest of my family members, my friends, and the people who believed in me.

I express special thanks to my publisher, Barath, my editor, Archana, and the rest of the team members who helped me accomplish my vision into reality, and then to all the readers of my first book.

BASED ON A TRUE STORY

I wondered why the idol of Radhakrishna fascinated her the most amongst all of the gods that we pray to. Later, I realized that it was because she was going to experience a similar love in her life. For most people, friendship has to happen before love, but for her, love happened followed by friendship. The idea of writing about them occurred when he divulged his drug addiction to her after many years. I heard he had transfigured into a hophead after his mother died. He was even admitted into a rehabilitation center and had to be fastened due to his irrepressible behaviour. He was illicit to having any visitors, and no one in his family really knew about this. He didn't dare to inform them that he landed into several backlogs, and some of his actions had caused her to step back and choose another path. She never turned back to remembering this day until one fine day, when he returned with his confessions. I realized that the lockdown was the best time to put pen to paper on this story, which is as illusionary as their existence.

PROLOGUE

After his second confession to her,
I wrote some lines on them:

Their love is insanely thoughtful.
They have no boundaries, no rules.
Those concerns and respect need not any.
They were in love the moment they looked at each other.
It grew and got nurtured with time and distance.
Later, that same distance became destiny,
which favoured someone else in their lives.
However, there can't be any situation to let that love go.
It continued like rivers flowing into the ocean,
and the ocean can never dry.
It is as pure as pearls inside the oysters
that are found into the depth of the ocean.
It is their unconditional love,
I describe.

DURING SCHOOL

Aizawl

Those were the early days of their PUC when they first saw each other at the entrance of the corridor. Well, the first meeting in life with anyone counts, especially those with whom you later get close, but these two love birds spent that year just enjoying each other's presence and stealing glances. That whole year must have felt like different versions of their meeting; the way they were stuck in this beautiful phase of experiencing love. They were raised in the same city of Aizawl. Fortunately, movies, social media, and news have today made most of the far-flung states of the North East familiar. Yes, that's exactly where I am sitting and writing this story for you to read and get carried away someday. And for those who aren't yet aware of this part of North East India, maybe I can take you on a short virtual tour through this story. By the way, it's a wonderful place. Who wouldn't like sightseeing the breathtaking beauties of these hills and valleys, which aesthetically resemble Shimla. Hey, you can always try excogitating a trip because a wish to arrive here isn't at the end of a rainbow.

Just like the grass that looks greener on the other side, hilly places are mesmerizing, and what's unknown is the risk involved for the livelihood here during the rains. Believe me! Rain is so consistent here that you may feel there hasn't been any other season. Of all the problems, landslides are the worst clouds on the horizon, a call to terrible nightmares sometimes, I should say. Anyway, the best period for a sabbatical is during Christmas, when you can enjoy the winter season and the occasion together.

This is also when you can expect the least amount of rain. So, you'll see people gathered around the bonfire, the natives' homes packed with guests, and people hogging on a variety of feasts. A couple of more interesting facts related to Christmas are that as and when the occasion is about to arrive, they shop exclusively with the budget that they have retrenched the whole year. Now, Aizawl bazaar is conceived as the most conventional agora in the city. You will find it hard to trace an inch to step your foot on as people from all over the state throng the place during this festival month.

Now that you are a little more familiar with Aizawl, let's get back to our story. Having been raised in the same city, they had almost similar reasons to land at the same School. In those days, CBSE had a huge value and out of the 2Schools that were affiliated with this board, they picked (MICE) Mizoram School of Comprehensive

Education, primarily because it was commutable. Their families were settled here for ages, especially hers, and the good thing was that they both had a fine grasp of Hindi, which surprisingly the native people here don't give a tinker's cuss about. Many Hindi-speaking families have migrated and got their feet under the table, just like mine. However, their skills in the language paid less benefit as they hardly spoke to each other in their 2 whole years of PUC.Can you believe it! I have never seen anyone being this timid at that age, and that too living in a state like Mizoram, where people are shamelessly expressive when it comes to passing comments or just speaking about anything they feel.

They are harsh with their words too at times. Dheeraj once got offended, and even she witnessed a furious side to him that day. The thing is that all the Non-Mizos like us are put in a section of 'vai'. The word originated from 'bhai' and as they couldn't spell or for that matter pronounce it correctly, they made it vai. For them the logic was simple, but growing up, we largely felt offended and humiliated to be addressed that way in place of our names, irrespective of the gender. Well, I was proud that they imbibed none of those characters, just like a lotus leaving its essence even in filthy surroundings. They acquired these admirable qualities at an early stage of their adulthood, when normally youth get influenced by what they're exposed to. Love and awkwardness never left their minds and this simply reminds me of the silent lovers of the 80s.

But one day, when they were passing by the entrance of our classroom, she seemed to have felt a strange energy and looked back at him. She continued looking until he looked back at her. She was later blushing for getting arrested to stalk. The coincidence was so beautiful, maybe because they purposely stole glances after that. She was actually coming into the classroom to attend a Biology class, and he was heading out after a Math class that she had omitted. Now, in the middle of the year, he began taking Hindi just to be able to stare at her. They were literally the 'talk of the School', as if they were having an affair. The rumour spread like a fire due to one of our cruel batchmate's maliciousness. He was not only our batchmate but his neighbour and close friend in School. As for her, her aunt who was studying in the same School was of utmost concern.

There were around 12 Non-Mizos in the class, and some tended to underestimate her for not taking Math. Her father was a Math teacher and that had led them naturally expect her to pick the subject; she understood that but never really cared to respond back. If the subject had anything to do with anyone's intelligence, even broadly, then she was admissibly a non-genius. How astute, she thinks of them now, anyway. However, Dheeraj's attitude towards her was different. She never heard him gossip or unnecessarily comment. He wouldn't speak unless he felt strongly about anything, and she liked the way he silently stood by her.

He was intelligent, sensible, and good-looking, qualities that she admired in men but was also extremely shy and reclusive. She was never swayed by his looks alone; his overall personality was what attracted her in those days. He was tall and dark yet his complexion didn't matter to her as long as his features were sharp. She didn't know what relationships meant in sooth, but having these kinds of rumours spread all over about her affair with him made her feel as though they were a couple in real life. Learning Hindi appeared to be a work cut out for him, we could see. She was wondering why he had to drop Biology. Though he was fluent in speaking Hindi, his confidence shook when it came to theory, and she thought maybe that's why he had picked the language; to learn it properly.

The classroom was spacious, so he would scoot to the back bench and sit alone. He would choose a place from where it was convenient for him to watch her slyly, although he kept a poker face upfront. They were close-mouthed, shy, and reluctant. One day, when she lifted her eyes to peek at him, he pretended to talk to that same batchmate, who was sitting right next to him that day. She could sense that he had been looking at her right before that. She caught him many times after that, but they never stayed with their eyes fixed on each other like they had on the first day. Neither of them was taking a gander. Now, she was able to talk to almost everyone in the class except him.

As a teenager, teasing lances your feelings and it's easy to fall into this trap when one is as young and vulnerable as them. Maybe this caused her to feel awkward to initiate speaking at all, whereas he clearly had his neighbour-friend cum batchmate to blame for that. Anup, his batchmate, who was originally from Bihar, must have been some kind of queer for sure, we used to think. His feminine gestures were prudent and he enjoyed being flanked by both boys and girls. He would find reasons to sit with the girls and gossip during the break hour. Somehow, he also managed to find time to discreetly spy on them because they were his main interest, apart from his studies.

2005

By the time we reached the 2nd year of our PUC, Dheeraj came to understand that even she stole glances at him. As the days progressed, she became sure that Anup was manipulating Dheeraj's fiddlestick mind. Being his neighbour, it was darn easy to be incessantly around him and brainwash him. Anup could have had feelings for Dheeraj; we doubted why he would otherwise repeatedly stir his own mind and attempt to deter Dheeraj from approaching her in any possible way. From then on, she began to hate their companionship. Anup knew their intruding shyness and diffident youth could make them feel even more awkward to take their love further in School. Well, one of them had to initiate, and she moved heaven and earth to do it. Prema was Nepali. Though a little reserved, she was very gutsy when it came to taking a stand for the truth. She valued relationships and never shied away from expressing what she felt.

She couldn't go with the flow, waiting for things to change on their own. They were not even friends till this time, but she wanted to make some progress on their unnamed relationship. So, the desire ensued to buy him a birthday card, precisely a red rose, and a friendship band. To him, it looked like she had proposed a friendship and a relationship both at once, but for her, she just wanted him to start behaving like a friend, at least without reflecting any kind of hesitation. Somehow, she summoned up her guts and handed over those gifts when he was standing outside the Biology laboratory with one of our other batchmates named Nilesh. After she entered the lab and gave him the gifts, he hastened to the classroom, overwrought, and slipped them into his bag before anyone could see.

Anup couldn't seem to digest the love and friendship she offered to Dheeraj because he spoiled the fun very precariously, playing with Dheeraj's fiddlestick mind again. She couldn't believe that Dheeraj would be this cuss otherwise. His behaviour per se was the evident that her suspicion was indubitably true. Anup's ploys were only making her hatred for himself rise. Dheeraj never received proper guidance in his adulthood because he rested his trust on the wrong companion, and utterly failed to recognize that. Between them, there was only one person who genuinely cared for him.

Madhavan was a common friend and another South Indian batchmate in our group of Non-Mizos. Dheeraj was from Kerala and Madhavan was from Andhra. He was above the board and concerned about Dheeraj. However, he was also called dunce, a little underrated for having a record of sporadically failing in exams. Dheeraj neither encouraged nor discouraged anybody. Madhavan once spilled in front of Prema that Dheeraj wouldn't speak about her, and when asked, he put his foot down, refusing to accept that he loved her. In fact, he said her love was unrequited. He edified Dheeraj, saying that he could see his love for her crystal clear and that he must confess rather than try to deceive himself. Right now, his mind was closed to this matter, but he should let his feelings be heard before it's too late.

When Prema heard these things about herself, she broke down. As fate would have it, Dheeraj's mother was diagnosed with cancer, and at the same time, her father ceased to live. Madhavan felt that he must be insecure and stressed by that terrible news, but also felt it was his responsibility to make Prema aware of his status. "Maybe his responsibility towards his family and the upcoming board exams are making him feel so stressed that he isn't able to handle it. Maybe he only wants to concentrate on his studies as of now," Madhavan enunciated to her. She knew Dheeraj was not what he purported, but she was pounding. Her father's demise on the other hand took her to experience an emotional disaster during this time. In that state, she preferred to ignore him and had the propensity to do that.

Between Madhavan's sister, our junior in School, who had a secret crush on Dheeraj and Anup, the whistleblower, came dusting the dirt. I wonder what joy he got in her misery. Considering the time he chose to leak the news, it only seemed as if he just wanted to distort her mind somehow. He would spare no chance of making her feel insecure, which she had now become. Dheeraj usually hung at Madhavan's place, and Jaya, Madhavan's sister, was a pretty South Indian girl. So, according to her, she weighed more attention and deserved to be favoured. One day, after tuitions, we decided to join our batch's gathering at Madhavan's home, which was on the way. Prema took her chance and politely barged into his sister's room when everyone was having breakfast. She started off by asking about Jaya's studies and other things in School. Then, she slowly moved on to his topic, trying to talk some sense into her. The glow on Jaya's face, her wringing hands, and the way her eyes blinked, signified her ongoing massive feelings for Dheeraj. She was checking if she needed to apprise her of anything. When Jaya said it herself that she had heard about their affair, she didn't feel the need to tell her anything.

Prema was close-knit with 2 people in School – one was me and the other one was a Chakma guy named Ronak, who was a year junior to us. A while after they met in School, he started appearing in her house, often uninvited. I guess that's how she drew more affection toward him. He had a cunning and calculative mind, which I believed was a gift of a gene, having been hailed from an ex-MLA family and being a fine chess player. Alas! We could never stand each other and neither did she try to befriend us. Let me tell you that the Chakmas share the same tribal community in Mizoram, but they follow the religion of Buddhism, unlike Mizos, who follow Christianity. This community lives in one of the 7 districts in Mizoram named Chawngte, which is reserved for them. This was the only reason his father could govern the state at one point.

Prema's father had tragically passed away right then, and the whole class along with the principal and class teacher had shown up for the funeral. She would have roughly scrutinized everyone who came through the course of the mourning. Dheeraj didn't bother if he was on the watch for not being able to take his eyes off her. He had gone off the deep end that day and was watching her actions silently. The same fear must have hovered around his mind for his deceased mother, I felt that day.

2006

Months after her father passed away, Ronak started appearing in her house again. They were just reconciling over rejecting his puppy love proposal when he took the risk of fixing a blind date with his friend, Veeru, who was originally from Assam, for which she bent out of shape. She refused to meet him and proceeded home immediately after class. Now in the hills, the roads are never straight and as she walked up the slope, she saw someone dark and hefty waiting near the bus stop. She was completely spaced out and happened to stand there for a while when Veeru managed to catch a side of her. There was no room for escape unless she walked off but she preferred to sit with him and listen to exactly how he fell for her, where he first saw her, and all that. She had never seen him before, however, he had seen her in one of the events where he was performing. He was a struggling musician and a student in St. Paul's in those days.

Ronak now started appearing at her house in Veeru's company, and always had some feeble excuses for being at her place. His friend then began coming on his own, such that once, after celebrating her surprise birthday party that was organized by them, her old fangled grandmother dished out, "Where flower beats." Somehow, females are always the ones to be blamed even if the males are after them. Ronak would switch to the MTV channels; he was brawn and had no brain to feel any awkwardness while gazing into bare bodies when her mum was around. And Veeru, who I now call a dark guy, chased her wherever possible. He would bend and touch her grandmother's feet, so he wasn't that much on the hate list of the elders in her family. It was the night of Christmas when she turned down his invitation to a Bombay viking's concert that he came helplessly near her house. He had gifts and an autographed card with her name written on it to propose friendship to her. Because she didn't want to keep him in the dark, she declared her love for Dheeraj without taking his name. He must have heard things about Dheeraj from his dear friend, Ronak. Within a few days, she figured that he had dropped into the School with his uniform on, just to check on Dheeraj.

She was just packing her bag to leave when Ronak came inside the classroom to inform her that his friend was waiting. She quickly scrambled to the balcony and from where she was standing, she could see Veeru waiting in the shop. On the other side, Dheeraj was walking towards the class. She felt something murky about Dheeraj, the way he picked up his bag and stalked off. Her eyes were following him until he disappeared. It became very easy to make out that very moment what the dark guy had come to inspect. In this prospect, it's hard for a man to take ignorance and rejection. One of the days, Veeru even went to Ronak's place to vouch for her relationship status. Maybe he couldn't believe that he had really missed the boat. This time, Ronak quite pragmatically suggested seeking an answer from the horse itself.

I assumed Veeru had already given up on her because he stopped following her thereafter, or he must not have had the temerity to show up. Anyway, she was debilitated from life after her father's demise. She told me that there were hardly any savings left and that they had mere pension amounts collectively on the rim for their household and education to run as well as foster. She was so tense and depressed that she lost all interest in studies. She couldn't pay the kind of serious attention that one should before board exams. Nevertheless, a few weeks later, we arranged a small get-together before we all parted ways, which was held at my place. On that day, almost everyone in the Non-Mizo group had turned up except Dheeraj. This really upset her and I somehow convinced her to be in the moment. I wouldn't deny that the day was well-spent even with the others' presence after she made up her mind.

However, she screwed up in her boards and got compartment in her result. Instead of just attempting the 2 papers in which she had flunked, she decided to repeat the class simply because in those days percentages mattered a lot. But I didn't do that; I gave my compartment exams and started readying myself for the state entrances. Everyone else had passed, and Dheeraj had left for Kerala much earlier. Sadly, our principal behaved as if Prema asked for his pair of kidneys when she went along with her mum to seek his approval. All she wanted to do was attend regular classes, whereas he was instigating her to get married. Her mum then lost her cool and got knocked sideways. Eventually, her mum was reduced to tears when he added that she had had enough time to prepare for the exams. Prema couldn't agree any less with what he blamed her for, but what she couldn't see was her mother falling apart and begging for her seat. Our principal had no compassion and she was someone who wouldn't encourage any kind of sympathy, so she said thank you and left with her mum.

Later, we even heard that Dheeraj was pursuing his Engineering in Kerala, but she didn't contact him for a year. The last she saw of him was during the board exams, when he trespassed into the other room as his registration number was much ahead of her, alphabet-wise. Who would have known that the encounter would feel like a ship passing in the night for her because they never saw each other again. She was knuckled down to clear all her papers in a stretch. It took a year for her to get accustomed to talking to old friends and bounce back to a normal life. Further, she got hooked on to physics tuitions and there she bumped into the dark guy again. Unfortunately, they were in the same batch. He was speaking out of turn as to how she could fail in a subject like Chemistry. Even though she found his question utterly rubbish, she remained mum. She was reticent by nature, and especially with someone like him, she avoided speaking unless necessary. She was surprised to find him off the rails throughout their tuition.

2007

I had already moved out. Prema had passed her boards with flying colours and we were together till we prepared for our medical and para-medical entrances. I was Dheeraj's classmate from Merry Mount School, so had known him better and she was comfortable discussing her personal matters with me. I was the only one by her side, counselling perfect actions. I told her that being free from the kind of friend circle he had in School, there were chances of him slowly transforming into a different person. I only wanted to push her to make a new start by any means, but I guess I had already hit the nail on the head. "Yes, I must let down my ego and give it a try," she asserted.

The next day, she took his number from Madhavan and called him from the PCO booth. Dheeraj must have been in his 2nd year at that time. She had to plan and find ways to step outdoors; she would save her pocket money just to be able to have enough privacy while talking. It made her flesh crawl every time she called his number. She used to jot down whatever she was going to say to whip herself into shape. Both of them were timorous as they had never interacted before. They were going to have a conversation for the first time, and talking to him was as difficult as preparing herself for a visit to the dentist. In the course of time, gifts and letters were dispatched. His mother passed away in the middle of his 2nd year, and she didn't know how to console him. Having said that, she also wanted him to realize that she would stand by him no matter what. So, she spoke of her own experiences, thinking they would help as he knew that she resonated with his pain. She averred just how rued she felt when she had lost her father. She even quoted, "Mishaps and setbacks are an inevitable part of life," and that sometimes it's a wee bit that someone talks about something that stays forever.

I surmised that they had a heart-to-heart conversation that day.

She was following her father's dream and it was among his deepest desires to see her become a 'Nurse' someday. That was fed into her head, and she had nothing else in her mind. She had no clue as to what it was going to be like to become a Nurse when she embarked on this journey. Medical and Engineering degree courses caught most of the attention in those days, and she did what her father reckoned. The state had around 12 seats allotted and only females were eligible to enrol in the course. Her name was on the waiting list, so her mother helplessly went down on her spirit inside the counselling room when she was offered another course as an option. Her life was churning in another direction; she was going to pursue a normal degree like her mum suggested till the waiting lists were cleared. She could not see herself continuing that normal degree because nothing was precise as to what she was going to do after that.

Meanwhile, she and Dheeraj were duly speaking and I was not very impressed with his introvert personality. He was quietly accepting her gifts, enjoying her care and attention without reciprocating, so I told her to stop entertaining him. It was high time that she either have clarity about his feelings or move on in her life, otherwise, she would only end up getting hurt. He may never even express himself if she carried on this business. She needed to be practical and question him so that she came out of this whole world of delusion, if what she was thinking was merely going to be a part of it, I profoundly told her.

A few days later, I don't know what occurred to her but she went to meet Dheeraj's brother, our senior in School who worked as a substitute teacher for some time. He noticed that she was rooting with her eyes for someone outside the staff room and came to investigate. She just mentioned the crux of the matter before asking if they could sit somewhere and talk. They ate and conferred for about an hour. She told him without mincing any words that she loved his brother. She also brought to his knowledge that they had been in touch all this time but he still hadn't voiced anything. Maybe to light up the atmosphere with his frivolousness, he soon began flirting with her. When she paid no heed, he became seriously involved in the matter. He averred that they were poles apart and this was clear as a bell to her. Bhaiya recounted their upbringing, how different their basic natures were and how their parents had a love marriage.

They belonged to different religions but the same state, and that's why their marriage was possible, he confirmed. After tipping off relevant details about their family, he asked her to confront her feelings toward Dheeraj and get a clear picture of what was in his mind. He stated that their oneness may not be possible, considering all the differences they have. When his guess was as good as hers, he spouted that concentrating on her studies would be the ideal thing to do in the oncoming time. She sensed a knockback from him already and was as quiet as a millpond, creeping into sadness all the way home. As soon as she returned home, she quickly changed her clothes and flung herself onto the bed to shed all her tears on the pillow. She kind of offloaded all her emotional baggage onto her pillow that day.

AFTER SCHOOL

Bangalore

I was not convinced by the kind of course offered by the state. Like bad things come in 3, I was stuck with the same kind of resentment as before, so I decided to move to Delhi and Prema moved to Bangalore. As an act of adieu, she gave me a farewell treat a few days before we parted at the very restaurant where she had met bhaiya, where we used to hop usually. It was just the two of us that day, rewinding our old memories for the last time. She was traveling this long and far by train for the first time. It was her longest halt and the break journey was completely enervating, she told me. She started living with her uncle and two of his friends, who knew each other for a long time. In fact, one of them named Keshav, originally from Patna, was her uncle's School friend and was well-known to her. As the institute St John's was listed under the top 10, they recommended trying there foremost. She waited to contact Dheeraj till she was preparing and giving her exams. When she did not make the cut, that's when they started hunting for other Colleges and all of them accompanied her.

On weekdays, when everyone was in the office, she would spend time learning to do the chores, taking care of the kitchen, and learning to cook. She was struggling to be a caregiver for them. Her favourite part was cleaning the house and arranging things, which she was absolutely good at, but it didn't really satisfy the kind of people she was living with. This used to make her feel uneasy; because she was already miles away from her home and family for the first time. Sometimes, her uncle would pester Keshav to take her out when he would be busy with his night shifts. Otherwise, she had to wait for the weekends when she would get the opportunity to hang out in their company and have fun. Part of her homesickness was gone by spilling everything to Dheeraj on their calls. Now that she had a phone, it was quite easy to reach him whenever possible. Sometimes, he would call her from his end to get updates from her, and that's when they actually came closer.

It took a while for her to adapt to everything; she had lost her appetite for about a week after arriving there. Initially, she was even afraid to step out of the premises on her own, but slowly she picked up on the culture and lifestyle of the city. While she was learning to adjust, he was the only friend she had. In the midst, she was also learning to handle a man who found her irresistible. He was none other than her uncle's own friend, Keshav, who was a little less occupied as he was in a sort of break from work and at home. She was naive, vulnerable, uncomfortable, and petrified. She didn't know how to keep him away as they were living under the same roof. The only way she could figure was to lock herself in the bedroom whenever it was just the two of them. It was hard to avoid a person in a house as small as theirs. His intentions were getting filthy. He would barge into her room striving for some kind of physical contact. She had stopped watching television or doing anything that would make him appear next to her. She intended to keep herself secure no matter what it took to do that.

This went on for a month and then finally she opened up to Dheeraj, who then was all set to leave for Bangalore. He asked her to tell her uncle everything but she was concerned about their long and strong friendship. In fact, she did not want to spoil their friendship or weaken their bond. Before he knew all this, he seemed to have given her open clues about a girl named Rima in his College who he was very fond of. He initially diverted the topic every time she tried expressing her feelings, and finally one day, he disclosed his feelings for some batchmate that he liked. She could not believe a thing that he was saying or didn't want to understand the reality at all. However, she continued speaking to him despite knowing that bitter fact. Then on, he started speaking about Rima on his own and took great pleasure in her jealousy. He knew her investigation was entirely a part of her jealousy, more than the fact that she couldn't believe he could really love someone else. Her mind was so clouded by this made-up girl that she missed out on seeing how desperate he was to meet her and save her from the situation she had fallen into. She just asked him to stay where he was and that she would handle everything without him.

However, those insecurities settled down after Keshav realized her lack of interest in him. His behaviour was not comprehensive enough and she was glad that he corrected himself. The air in the house was clear now and the hatches were buried for both of them to get along there on. What didn't settle was her mind from believing that Dheeraj was already in love with someone else. She was insecure that their affair could begin anytime behind her back. Things may sparkle between the two of them once he let his heart out in front of Rima. Her worries took her to question everything about that girl; she again missed focusing on the similarities with her.

Weekends were days when she would love to forget everything and be around her uncle and his friends. Being the youngest, she was cosseted among her uncle's friends' circle. The early hour shows every Monday morning at PVR was much awaited by her. Sometimes, they would seek her opinion about the kind of movies they should watch, otherwise she walked into the theatre hall mostly blank about what she was going to watch. However, the thrill was beyond anything for a movie buff like her. Playing UNO was another favourite pastime, and just like that, the time to leave for hostel finally arrived. Since they were her only family back there, she got a group photo of them framed, which I believe she still carries wherever she goes.

But she still didn't have any memory of her and Dheeraj's stored, and that kind of bothered her at times. She only had the group picture of us in School, which she kept enclosed in a diary, the first thing that she bought in this city. He never spelled out that he loved her and she failed at catching his clues. She felt that if she was not crazy about him, there were fat chances of any progress in their unnamed relationship. But now they had one, they were friends for a lifetime. Her uncle's friend tried giving her a hard time again when she was no longer living with them. He would spy on her and investigate her whereabouts. She was afraid he would kick up a fuss about her personal matters, so she started visiting them a little less. He was someone who could become unpleasant at any time so she asked Dheeraj not to call her suddenly like before, as he had spotted her talking to him at times. If she was there during her vacation, she had to wait in the wings to have the pot luck of talking to Dheeraj. So, he would call her sometimes and drop messages whenever he wanted to talk to her or maybe even when he missed her. She would note all his actions, which spoke of him being besotted with Prema.

He was much more expressive now; I only wished that he had been a little more open about his feelings to his lady love. Despite telling him bluntly, he never confessed and she couldn't figure how else to enunciate. She was clearly dumb and new to this world of love, so this time when he spoke to her about Rima from his College, it just felt like he gave her a cold shoulder. Out of comity, she expressed an instant concern for his happiness and tried to fake her happiness too. Ever since, it had always given her a brain spin thinking of him with Rima. To her it seemed as if she was the one lovesick for him. She was brooding overnight with many other thoughts.

She was thinking, what if he had concocted everything to simply check her out? After that day, he wittingly raised the topic to either seek her advice or just to annoy her. She was so taken by all this that at one point, she started advising him with a heavy heart to propose to that girl before he loses her like she lost him. She was conveying her doleful condition at his loss. Something about that girl riveted her, but she was also wallowing in her sadness before she got over him completely. She mulled over many things before she spoke to him again. She was wondering if she had made an impression of a maniac, such as someone who is obsessed with him. Was she really forcing herself on him? If he really loved the other girl then why hadn't he informed her earlier? Why did he accept all her gifts? All these questions hung onto her but having been a slight introvert, it held her back from giving him the third degree. She was heartbroken so she stepped back and limited herself to friendship.

She desisted calling him though she never avoided his call. Now, she wanted to see his level of interest and endeavour in maintaining their friendship. At one point, she even wondered if she had committed a grave mistake of pushing him toward Rima. With the kind of attitude shaped in her, he may deem she was willing to let him go. She then consoled herself with the choice of fate. She accepted being his friend without any equivocation. He imposingly made more calls to compensate for hers, but in a reasonably short span, he began distancing himself from her. He gently reduced his frequency of calls, and she thought he must be busy with his girlfriend. Once he averred that he had almost proposed to Rima. He had bought a red rose because he had planned to bend down on his knees but dropped the idea in acute agitation. That moment she was trying to make him understand by saying that things would happen when they're meant to, and to not give up on Rima if he really loved her and all that. Silly girl was just unaware that she was only making things hard for him to come close to her.

2009

Like they say, the world is small. Most of the little gang of Non-Mizos we had in School were studying in the South, including the Chakma guy, Ronak, and his fatso friend, Veeru. They were all reaching out to her, even some who she had hardly interacted with had called her. She found that gesture very endearing as she had none of their numbers stored in her phone. In fact, I was the one furthest, studying biotech up North. Suresh, the topper of our batch, originally from UP, was smart yet sensitive enough to get caught between us. He saw me as his sister right from the beginning but I was her best friend. Because he did not want to get into the wrong frame by being partial to her, he insisted that she tie him a rakhi when she had clearly vented her lack of interest in forming a name-sake relationship. Suresh dragged her into this affair and she finally had to tie the rakhi. Ever since, she has continued to send him a rakhi, pressed inside a greeting card.

There was not a single soul who didn't call and show the slightest botheration about hers and Dheeraj's lives; everyone was interested in knowing what they were really up to now. Our School friends had grown up a bit now that they had stepped out of the place they were raised in. None of them were awkward speaking about anything openly, they were accepting their execrable behaviours and confessing the unknown. They were building and uprising their characters, overcoming their callowness, and putting in harnesses to becoming real adults. They were exposing probably unheard facts about Dheeraj because she still appeared mad keen to them. They had been persons of interest in School but had eyes only on each other. Therefore, she preferred to keep matters secret and personal, letting everyone know that they had become real friends now. Dheeraj called her less often, but they were updated about each other until she reached the middle of her 2nd year. She left the hostel and started staying as a paying guest.

Another fact that she couldn't take was having Dheeraj disappear all of a sudden without any intimation. She let go of her ego and tried calling him many times. This was the turning point of her life because she also met someone when he was away. Dheeraj was supposed to be graduating that year as he was already 2 years ahead of her. She was curious and hard-headed, so she broke the vow she had made to herself of not calling him. He absconded for more than a year, meaning she had now reached her 4th year when he finally sent her an SMS. She had taken a back seat by then and ensued to remain in a state of oblivion for long.

2010

She had met this new guy named Faiz, who she called the love of her life. He lived in a flat close to where she stayed as a paying guest, so they went for a walk almost every day after their classes, much like in the movie 'A Walk to Remember'. He was a batchmate of her roommate, an Assamese girl named Noyoni, who was studying Engineering. Faiz was from Raichur, Karnataka. He was tall, good looking, and intelligent, and more than that, he was her best friend. They just needed tickets to be with each other that time, and she would tell me that he revelled in watching her eat delightfully whenever they were out. After a year of friendship, they promptly slumped into a relationship and required no more excuses to spend time. While she was just beginning to enjoy her love life, Madhavan called her to discuss his own issues with his girlfriend. He was then doing an internship in one of Gujarat's construction companies. He was the only one who had never called her before that, and this time he did because he wanted some tips to sort his messy love life. School friends can be mean and lovely together, they say, so she chucked and thought chalo, at least he remembered her somehow.

2011

At the same time, our cute bro Suresh was often there giving interviews with the idea of moving from Mangalore, where he was studying in those days, so she got to meet him sometimes. Dheeraj's text messages started coming regularly, and she was all excited to tell him about her boyfriend, Faiz. As she was also curious to know where he had been for such a long time, smack dab! She asked him that at first but he deferred it for later stating that "it was complicated." Since she was dying to unfold the news, in no time after that she opened up about her relationship. He was going to tell her something before that but she didn't wait. As she was speaking about her relationship, his girlfriend in College struck her instantly and she asked him unswervingly. He lied to her and said that he had gone to Rima's mother, but she didn't agree to their marriage. She refused to lock her daughter's hands with an unsettled man in withal. She popped off, if his job was the only concern, her mother could have waited, and why didn't his girl say anything? The way Rima just clammed up implies that it was okay for her to let him go.

He was still trying to put Rima in a good shoe by saying, "Maybe she couldn't utter anything in front of her mother, but that's okay. I am replaceable, it's no big loss for her and that's blatantly true. Walking away from her life was the best thing I could do since that day." She truly had a sinking feeling for him. Her mother's behaviour clearly substantiated that she weaved plans to shoo him off. Then on, she didn't validate his girl's value in his life as to her Rima didn't deserve him anymore. He might feel like she was adding fuel to the fire if she constantly hashed over Rima, so she changed the topic in a flash to cool him down. But for one thing, she was gratified that he had a job now.

2012

The next time he called, ironically, she was at her uncle's home again. Her uncle and his friend, Keshav were going to part ways. They had scraped through MAT and were now going to pursue MBA in different cities. Whereas another friend, she called Carol didi had already completed her MBA in the same city, so naturally she was the only one to be left at that house. Looking at the vast uncertainty of life, they counted on spending their last moments together. Another change that happened that day was Dheeraj feeling liberated while speaking with her on a call. They spoke for more than an hour for the first time. She was pleased to see this better version of him, who was far more approachable and extroverted now. This is how friendly she had always wanted them to be. They were becoming the best of friends with the passage of time, and she was much more composed.

On the other hand, her boyfriend was turning possessive day by day after their intimacy. He had half-baked trust in her and they split hairs for some common friend who had gifted her an instrument because she loved music. It was out of friendship, she knew that, but he had his mindset fixed. He was scared that his only friend, Rajiv would snatch her with his splendid gestures. He didn't want Rajiv to give any damn thing to impress his girlfriend and conveyed that implicitly one day over their arguments. The next day, when she returned it to Rajiv, he evinced that he had no ill intention as to what her boyfriend was suspecting. He asked her not to embarrass him by returning a gift that he had bought with so much adulation. Though Faiz brought that instrument back to her after this incident, he always fought with her for accepting it again. She was not used to big tiffs, especially the way he had escalated this one. She was getting exposed to many of his intolerable behaviours with the passing of time and this belligerent attitude was on top of the chart. Like they say, "Love is blind so one cannot love and be wise."

She even reached a point of breaking the instrument into pieces when there was no one in her room. She was not someone sullen who threw tantrums, despite that he was able to goad her into breaking the violin for his relief. She had actually been practicing sometime before that and the instrument was lying on the bed, so one can imagine his level of influence on just a call. She was mad as a hatter and wished to smash his head if he was around. She still counted this ridiculous action of hers as the biggest mistake of her life, a sin she could never be forgiven for. She had plans to venture into music but shot herself badly on her own foot. If he was a little cooperative and sensible, he could have prevented her forlorn hopes from getting dashed.

She took baby steps and began to familiarize him with her sisters, Rekha and Surekha, who were there for studies. She was thinking about unveiling the news at the right time, and in the interim, she wanted him to win their trust whereas no one at his home had even heard about her. Right when she started her internship, she had gone to meet him in Mysore, where he was undergoing training in INFOSYS. This time, she had to pay the price for allowing him to make a mistake because of which she became pregnant. Luckily, she had sorted her sister, Rekha's admission before all this could happen. A week before her final exams, she met with another accident wherein one of her hands were badly injured. It was at the reunion party of School friends when someone banged the door right when her hand was were at the edge, where the hinges are placed. She screamed in pain. The next morning, her fingers were bleeding and her right hand was found cyanosed. She couldn't lift her own hand without support. She didn't realize that the physical pain would get that intense when the mental pain of aborting a child was still healing. Her exams were falling up and that was her main concern, but she had to deal with all this by herself and couldn't even tell Dheeraj, who hadn't made it for the reunion that day.

DURING JOBS

Bangalore

She relocated to another area where she found a job and would have hardly had a gap of 6 months after her previous pregnancy. Her boyfriend had completed his training by then and was longing to meet her, so took her somewhere near the hospital she worked in to spend some time with her. She had just started her career and he got her pregnant again. She was earning peanuts; it was probably the end of the month and Faiz always relied on her for almost everything, so she didn't have a single penny to pay for the ultrasound. This time, she went straight for the scanning after she started experiencing sudden morning sickness. She escaped from the lab where she got to read the report of her pregnancy. She was already handling a sulky superintendent and the hostel was grotty. To top it all, it was her birthday when they went looking for a clinic far away from her hospital to get rid of the child she was carrying. She had spent the past 3 months working, while her classmates were at home, footloose and free post their exams. Without wasting anymore of her time there, she withdrew her last compensation and quit that job so that she could start a new life in a new area. With her sister, Rekha just having started her semester classes, she couldn't really make any plans of travelling to their hometown, so the poor girl chucked the idea of taking a vacation and joined another multi-specialty hospital.

2013

She had stowed all of her stuff at her uncle's house, so went straight there from the hospital's hostel. Before getting back to her normal work life, she fixed her main issue of getting an abortion done at a clinic in the same locality. This time too she had to deal with it all by herself. She then vacated their place and moved into a full-fledged working paying guest accommodation, which was an easy commute from her new hospital. Faiz and her schedules had now changed; they were gainfully employed and no longer lived in the same neighbourhood. Their relationship was taking a new course. They were paddling in their own canoes. However busy they were, they still managed to spare time for one another. She often gathered with her sister to meet her uncle's 3rd roommate, Carol didi, who was living alone after her uncle and Keshav had left the house. On one side, things were changing for the better and on the other side, happiness was fleeting. It was on the same day that she saw – through a FB post – Dheeraj's picture with his wife and his status changed to 'married'. She must have gazed at that picture for at least 5 minutes, trying to recall things from their last conversation. She did remember him saying that with the kind of frequency he chooses to call, the next time he called he may probably be married. She didn't understand whether his statement was ironical or alluding to the fact.

That night, she went back to brooding over many things. Maybe it was a shotgun wedding, maybe the girl was arranged by his family and he had tied the nuptial knot in haste. Maybe he had been dating her all this time. She thought of vindicating the truth later and left a simple comment, just "Congratulations!" The place where his wife stood in the picture was once what she had so envied and maybe still did. Those emotions were gushing; the dotted feelings were coming all at once, like the saying, "If love is a stormy passion, jealousy is its corollary." Later, she got busy planning her own life's boat.

2014

She was badly stuck with her final year backlogs, which somehow she couldn't clear in a stretch. Every time she applied for leaves, she would also book the train ticket with an idea of taking a break and going home for a week or so, but that never worked. On her third and final attempt, she had used all her piled up leaves for the exams and a trip home soon after that. Now it was possible to join the hospital under those circumstances in the initial year of practice. But she was yet to complete her registration at the Nursing Council, which makes it accomplished if you are in the profession. It is mandatory for every Nurse to have this done in the state they prefer to work in. But by the time she finished her exams, the season changed and it started raining. She had already cancelled her tickets twice before, so her mum's worries and denial on the call made her super upset. "It would be equal to putting yourself in a heap of risks to travel to a hilly state like this in the rainy season," her mum explained. Her mum's exhortation made sense to her in the end, and she postponed her homecoming for the 3rd time.

During this time, Faiz had already started plotting something. "My mum is ill," was the last message he had sent to her before heading to his native place. He flew the coop; she didn't hear him for 2 months after that. He was playing the mouse, and called her one day blabbing about how his family is trying to get him married. She didn't take him seriously at that time. He had taken the plunge on her birthday that same year. He had bought clothes and accessories, a beautiful bouquet, had her pet name printed on a cake, and had stood outside the hospital at 12 AM just to be able to wish her when she was on her night shift. All this was exceptional, that's why nothing really smelled fishy to her. She believed in him, believed that he wouldn't take any major step without discussing it with her first. Guess she was wrong; he finally rang her one day to let her know that his engagement was fixed. He had never tipped a wink on his plans for marriage with her. It was still unbelievable for her to have him turn his back on her like that. Her friends had forewarned her, but she was the one who had had blind faith in him, wherefore she paid heavily. He behaved like a rat who leaves a sinking ship because she was struggling with many things in her life at that point in time. Like they say, "Misfortunes happen once." He had proved his infidelity and cowardice together, which is why she blamed no one but herself for that ditch.

She was going through hard times back-to-back. She got back to an overly strict and grouchy superintendent with whom she had to join her nerves to face her every day. She was worried about her backlog results; she had her important registrations leaning on them. His engagement had already broken her from within. Her next job, where she was paid well and had no night shifts, was the only good thing that had happened to her in these times. She was tired of this whole episode, so stopped answering calls, meeting any friends, and wouldn't sleep without drinking.

Her life circled from work to paying guest accommodation, and she was never at rest; simply couched before the screen, entertaining herself. She kept herself occupied with co-curriculars like painting, sketching, and writing, which she used to enjoy. Once, when she was checking the inventory, she quietly wailed thinking the same. At that moment she realized that she was ravaging into a slow depression and it called for her to wake up. She no longer wanted to be that feeble again, so she made herself stronger by understanding that she had many things to look forward to. Anyway, everything started falling into place for her soon, and she could see a silver lining behind the cloud. She finally graduated, got her registration and

KNC certificate released, and was also rewarded with the best employee twice. In the middle of that same year, Dheeraj's first son was born. She saw their pictures together, which came up on WhatsApp, and he wanted her to name him. Now, this was supposed to be his and his wife's joint affair, but since he insisted, she suggested names from the alphabet that he preferred.

2015

This was the first time he had connected with her after she had come across his wedding news on Facebook. She was kind of used to his absconding by now, so didn't discuss anything much about her life. Around the same time next year, he forwarded pictures of his growing up son and his son enjoying doodling and sketching exercises. She knew he was superb at artwork and sketching, which he pursued in his leisure time. Every time he pinged, she would be at work, so the conversation mostly boiled down to a concise chat. However, that day, she could invest in chatting for a long time though she was in the hospital. Since they were anyway talking in reference to his sketching hobbies and his kid, so she pulled the topic towards their marriage nonchalantly.

He let on that his wife, Silvi, was simple and that she didn't interfere in his matter of choice and neither did he in terms of hers. He voiced his opinion only when he was asked, otherwise he was mostly indulged at work or with his kid. He also blithely invited Prema to

Kerala and said, "My wife and son would be delighted to meet you." She smiled and said, "Someday, for sure." Then he started revealing how their marriage had exactly happened. "It was neither love nor arranged, it was a situational marriage." Their families didn't get along for a year, thinking he was the guy Silvi was once going to commit suicide for, whereas he was the one who had saved her. His wife worked as a receptionist in the same College where he was a lecturer. She was in love with a pen-friend from FB. He always found her hooked either on calls or chatting with someone, but learned her story much later. One day, he spotted Silvi heading out with an airbag; she had planned to elope with that guy. He was just starting his bike and asked her out of curiosity when she explained her plan. Ill at ease, he dropped her to the station and waited until her guy showed up. That guy was supposed to pick her up from the station as per their plans, but he didn't even care to answer her calls.

Silvi felt highly scrupled going back home and facing her family as there had been heated arguments going on about that guy within her family for the past many days. Dheeraj still insisted that she return to her family, but she began crying vigorously. She envisaged that her image would be spoiled if her family got to know about the whole incident, and no one would marry her in the future. Then, she almost put her foot forward to jump on the tracks; this very incident changed his life forever. Now, he didn't want to be in trouble, so before things messed up and the police came over to create a scene, he quickly vowed to marry her. After this, it wasn't difficult to convince her to stay at his flat in Kochi, where he lived alone, which was some 8 hours away from his own house. That constant stick made him take a decision, and they got hitched within 7 days. His fate with her was then sealed. Prema didn't believe any part of that story for many years, except for the fact that her misconception about their arranged marriage had just got cleared.

Something within her said, "Silvi is not right for him." Yes, it's true, she never liked Silvi's face out of jealousy. She grew even more suspicious after she heard this story; she could sense that his wife had kept something under wraps. However, she didn't want to dig old graves thereupon. She was looking to pursue her Master after quitting that job and had plans of leaving the country by and by. She always felt thankful for getting the opportunity of touching many people's lives inside the hospital. She called her experiences classified and miraculous. Her last few days in this city were unforgettable; she was getting farewell treats from the MD the administration dept, and many more gifts from her colleagues and friends as she was leaving forever. Who knew that the other gift of a pen would change her fate, and her path would bloom like a bouquet, she received, in the coming days.

2016

She was deeply touched by what her MD had to say when she was about to leave his cabin post the farewell.

He felt she was going to be at the top of her game in the next 10 years. But the game changed after she returned to Bangalore. Things did not work out as planned, but like they say, "Life is what happens while you are planning something." She was working and giving M.SC exams when things in her life took a great turn. She had never stopped writing since her boyfriend had left; the best way she had found to pour her heart into when she was going into depression. Who knew that it would take her so far in her life? That's why they say, "When your heart is involved, you just keep doing things without thinking about anything and perseverance conquers all." That Doctor had lit high hopes in her that day. He believed that she would do something great, he may not have realized but his anticipation had done the job of enlightenment in her.

But things didn't come easy for her. Before all this could happen, she was tense at home; her mind was jammed because she never thought of staying there that long, and nothing was working according to her plan. She thought about investing money wisely, hence, she made a smart move. Studying in Bangalore was not going to cost her much, and on top of that, her mother was sponsoring, so she was even more careful when making decisions. She had avoided talking to friends while she was going through this torrid time. This hard phase stretched for 5 months and finally, she was a bit relieved after she could lay her plan into action. Dheeraj was the only one she was speaking to in those days, but after things got sorted for her, she got accustomed to many of her other friends.

Dheeraj had sent her pictures and it was his second child she was gaping at now. Again, he requested her to suggest a name for his 2nd son too, starting from the same letter 'T'. Didn't know why he had an obsession with that letter, she could never make out and neither did she ask. Also, she hadn't expected his 2nd child to be born this soon. It was only a year back that his 1st child had brooded. She had become quite outspoken having spent years in the city, but with him, she was a little meticulous. She wouldn't just throw it away.

But this time, they were beating their gums over the past events in School quite comfortably till midnight. Before that night, he never had the propensity of telling her how much he adored her. He was talking turkey on his level of admiration, fondness, love of companionship, and connectivity with her. Even she disclosed her past meeting with his brother in a trivial way. She was fine baring her heart as she had already recuperated. They had actually never vouchsafed that interesting titbit before. A week before returning to the city, she had knelt before the Lord, the supernatural power that is the inevitable cause of anything in this universe, and prayed that he spare her from the same kind of adverse misery and let her evolve as a better and stronger person. It looked like her prayers got answered differently. Poor thing, they had to undo the journey with the same old luggages, in fact, with much-loaded ones.

She had started living with her sister, Rekha and her sister's friends from her previous paying guest, who she was amicable with at a close range. They had rented a house after Rekha too had started earning. She joined a multi-speciality hospital where she was slammed with enough work. Night shifts were draining her energy while day shifts felt like a few days. It always needed some kind of mental preparation, endeavouring that right muscle to undergo nights at the hospital. When she finished her entrance for M.SC Nursing, which she was managing along with her job, she became unfettered by some work. She could resume her co-curriculars and get back to writing. She preferred solitude and space with no intrusion, but in a house packed with people, it would only be a daydream. Anyway, she had the practice of writing with paying guests' friends and their noises around. On the other hand, there was immense pressure from her ward HOD, who was impulsive, intricate, unfathomable, and bossy. She still perceived that he adored her although he was never partial to anybody. He seemed pleasant in the beginning when she had joined but with the passing time, she discerned his dictatorial behaviour. Though she was used to such unkind supervisors yet it started to become intolerable. Whenever she told the other staff that she was posted in the general ward, they would express their concern, and even break their legs. He was some kind of maniac for sure to everyone there.

It had actually taken a year for her to believe that she was going to become a Nurse back when she was studying and now the same thwarted feeling arrived in her again. She believed that it was her vocation to become a Nurse but she was also absorbed with the feeling that she was meant to do something else. She was kind, empathetic, and had enough humanity required to surrender herself in the service of others. The impulse was strong and she was being swept away. Maybe she started realizing that she could do great if she followed her passion after repeatedly hearing praises about her write-ups. Getting into content writing could very much help appraise and enhance her skills, is what some of her close ones and sister's friends were telling her. They were encouraging her to kick start with freelancing so that she didn't have to really leave her job.

One morning, her HOD blissfully invited her to join him for breakfast. Late that same afternoon, there was a complete shift in his attitude and he lashed out at her in front of a duty Doctor. He had an ugly record for his bad temper. He would yell at colleagues to prove his obedience, and had received a good shouting from the Director himself. She couldn't let him play the game of puppeteer of his mood anymore. She wanted to slap him on his wrist and she did just that; she wrote a resignation letter and dashed into her higher superintendent's cabin. That lady Nurse was aware of his misconduct, even then she was not willing to take charges of his offense. On the contrary, she was trying hard to save him. She asked Prema to come back after she had cooled down the next day and suggested that she could shift her to another ward.

Prema noticed that the lady Nurse had a soft spot for her HOD, which was making her behave that way. The lady Nurse attempted to keep things off the record, but the fire had already reached the jungle. She knew her sup's overbearing nature would not allow her to do what needed to be done, so she took the same copy and went to the Director's wife who was also a Doctor there. The lady Nurse would have put words in the Doctor's mouth after she left, so she was speaking her language the next day when she went there with her resignation letter. They were trying to settle the matter tacitly, placing Prema in some other ward instead of dealing with the culprit. So, the Doctor gave her a choice, either quit and forgo the salary or quietly accept the offer. But she rested the case plainly and advocacy was done in his favour without any effort from his side. He didn't have to do anything as long as that sup, in particular, was in his court. "I'm not here to be satisfied with any unwanted settlement; I have held him to your jurisdiction for no compensation but for justice and peace, once and for all," she spoke. Then, she picked the choice to quit and live with grace.

That day changed her life forever because she started applying for full time content writing job and then pursued Journalism in place of M.SC despite getting selected in the hospital where she had been rejected for B.SC once. In the meantime, she was tackling Faiz's comeback. His father deliberately broke his marriage due to mutual internal disputes with the bride's family. He quit his central government job at his native place and positioned him back into this city for her sake. He texted her not many days after that news. He was pretending to be married even then, but Prema was least bothered by his scheme. A week later, Faiz brought her up to speed with his current status. He was smart enough to find out about her whereabouts. She came to understand that he had obtrusively kept a track of her because within a month, he had found both her house and the hospital she worked in. She was surprised to see him waiting outside the hospital one day. She had just stepped out in the morning after her night shift, half asleep and stupefied and there he was, standing like an innocent child in front of her. She didn't care a hoot and made herself scarce by walking off to her flat. He was spotted at the same place the next morning too.

Though she was worn out and groggy, she still had a bone to pick with him. They were strolling through a park in the hospital's neighbourhood, then sat down on a bench, apart from each other. She gave him his own sweet time to talk, letting him serve his purpose of being there. He was feasting his eyes on her and she didn't even bother to glance at him. She brusquely told him to be quick as she needed to rest after 24 hours of being awake. By now, she had learned the art of making her worth and grants count from her previous experiences. He was looking to make the conversation happen by talking superfluously. Soon, he gave up his act of normalcy and broke down into tears. He came to the point of making a confession and asking her out. She wanted to allow him to express himself comfortably before arriving at any kind of resolution. So, she replied that she would go home and take a nap before she douched and changed for lunch.

Later in the afternoon, they stomped into her favourite cafe where he ordered her treasured dessert. He always enjoyed watching her eat delightfully, which lent him some level of satisfaction and gave him a lift, which was displayed in his eyes and gestures. While she was still eating, he clasped her hand and said, "I am working on getting you back into my life. I want to walk down the aisle with you." She scowled right then and spouted that being with him wouldn't implicate her interest. He was supposed to ascertain her will before putting forth his idea of marriage. With him, there was no denying that she was in 7th heaven for her. She would get ready with her bells on yet it was hard to pull her back at once. They were in touch and at least hung out frequently. They were having a whale of a time but she also had to keep her eyes open to the facts and not burn her fingers again like a fool.

Now, after all this, he dared to drop her a message where he mentioned,"It might not be possible for us to be together." That flipped her wig and though he rushed back to rectify his mistake, she kept on ignoring his countless calls. He still knew how to pull a few strings. Like always, he showed up at her colony, trying to turn her helpless by showing chocolates and movie tickets, targeting her sweet weaknesses. Then, he took her to the theatre directly, this way she wouldn't refuse and it would help him blow her steam beforehand. "Silence is more dangerous." She did not say a thing that evening and this bothered him more. He came abreast of everything in the next couple of days. But from the moment she had read those messages, she was at her wit's end, so she longer wanted to entertain his selfish ideas and bypass his crooked mind. Before he could say anything she exclaimed, "Why did you have to come back into my life if you hadn't for real changed your heart? You have destroyed my peace of mind and brought me back into dire straits. The breach in our relationship is not as easy to fix as it seems." She gave him the real talk.

He then spilled his guts and said, "I am unfortunately at a crossroad from where I cannot choose between my family and you, though I really want you." She took his words with a grain of salt because he was acting as if he was really stuck between a rock and a hard place. A few weeks later, he dropped by her house, trying to grab a chance of sexual congress. It's true his presence had made her heart grow a deepest fondle. She was yearning to make love as much as he was, still, she couldn't be disgraceful by inviting him when no one was in the house whereas in lieu she was warming up to his idea of checking into a hotel.

He caught hold of her when she was heading back from her duty. She was not at his beck and call like she used to be. That's because she knew that things would be back in the saddle and their oneness would punch her hard on the Achilles' heels. She was waiting with bated breath herself and yet she sat on the fence for some time. Anyway, he couldn't be any happier with the way the ball had bounced because she had agreed to it at last. They were making love after 2 years, baring their soul to each other, fulfilling their earnest longingness by unreservedly emoting their intense love. Their chemistry entailed huge emotions, causing a stir to passionate love and sending shivers down their spine even while they were just laying down caressing and cuddling each other in bed. "This was one of the many things I have missed out on, I can't feel the same again with any other woman," he vented. She was pleased and in heaven for an hour before they had to vacate the room. She was unsure if she would get the chance of loving him again, whether her fate would have him forever or that moment was just going to be a fluke. Hence, she hugged him tightly for a long time and was not even ready to leave his arms. Furthermore, he became uncertain and unforeseeable, blurting out that they may have to part ways. That tugged at her heartstrings. He was reopening the old wounds, but she knew she had to be strong and prepare for whatever happens in the future. At that point, she knocked him back, shifted to one side and squealed. She couldn't even speak because of the heavy lump in her throat.

During PG

Bangalore

Anyway, the day she left the hospital, she was feeling blue, but someone in the house, one of her sister's friends named Niharika had been a mover in her life. She was always by her side with her seldom words of wisdom. She chaperoned her most of the time and took care of her in many wondrous ways. She insisted on applying for full-time content writing, which she did and later pursued her M.A in Journalism and Mass Communication whereas Rekha pursued her M.SC Electronics and they both landed in the same College. Niharika was the one who instilled the idea of presence and benevolence in her sister even before she received a wonderful gift of a violin again after 6 long years. Once, before she got into Journalism, she even had her counsellor, who was originally from Assam, refer to Shakespeare and say, "Writers are self-made and their talent is inborn. You need not study any course to become a great writer. You can be dual and exponent, can very well choose to remain a Nurse and equally befit into a Content Writer. The course will only help you explore if you are keen on making a full-time career in writing." She was impressed by her counsellor's genuine approach. Then, Prema and Rekha had to shift nearer to the College and rented another house.

She was up with her eyeballs and had her 1ˢᵗ semester exams coming up when her ex-boyfriend, Faiz started calling her again. After he failed to persuade her with his endless calls, he appealed to their mutual friend, Junaid, because he knew she wouldn't leave Junaid's call unattended. He even knew that she was purposely ignoring his calls. It was the seed of insecurity planted by her that was now sowing out; the more she ignored it, the more it grew. But like they say, drastic times call for drastic actions. Junaid conveyed his idea of marriage to her and pressed to have some words with him. By then, Faiz's call was already on wait and he had become very impatient. He came back screeching like a wet cat unabashed. As she answered his call, he popped the question without any delay. When she turned down his proposal, he cried convulsively. She didn't melt at his wail, though she was hearing him cry out loud for the first time. In fact, she told him to get back on the call once he was done. She was damn cold and wouldn't let his emotions countenance her.

She wasn't willing to backflow with him, and he was not ready to believe it unless she agreed to refuse in front of him. She was aware of his concealed wily intention; how he wanted her to rant and rave beside him. He was also trying hard to please her because this time he wanted to save their relationship, as he couldn't lose her at any cost. He had started working in Chennai and came down on weekends to meet her. He was the best version of himself now. He had come a long way to be with her forever, despite that her mind was puzzled and her heart was sinking in emotion. Again, she didn't want them to be seeing each other without recognizing the possibilities of marriage. She wanted to be sure of his plans and the fact that he would execute them.

2017

He exposed his wish of settling with her in the Middle East in the near future. He had also made plans to elope after her Post Graduation. She felt pea-brained and gullible of herself here. After listening to that, she didn't find anything worth compromising for their relationship's sake. After all, he had left her in the lurch and only she had to bear the brunt emotionally, physically, and mentally. She had had enough patience with him and had rendered enough chances already. That being the case, she put him on the spot on her birthday. He had forcibly bought her new clothes the day prior and had also bought movie tickets in advance. Half of her day was gone in him convincing her to hang out with him. She cooperated eventually and headed out without being much of a spoilsport. It was after the movie, when they sat to grab their lunch, that a deep conversation took place between them. He coughed up, "I am still sliding between you and my family, which is why I felt that eloping was the safest plan in the beginning. This would put my family under obligation. They will not have the temerity to disown me completely, maybe at a snail's pace, but they will be driven towards us on the grounds of blood ties. I have in fact foreseen a 2BHK flat at my native place." At that moment, she appreciated his honesty but not his morals.

She deplored his plan and averred sternly, "If at all you want to marry me, you would have to ask my mother in person and the customs would take place in the presence of our family members and not otherwise." She quit the old habit of leaving him a handful of options. He then came apart at the seams and started requesting her to give him some time. She had asked him to decide by the end of her 2nd semester, which meant he had precisely 4 months left. But after the counselling of one of her close friends and an earlier roommate, Ayesha, who belonged to the same community and was in fact, living a few kilometres away from Raichur, rang her up and called a spade to spade, she changed her mind. Ayesha told her, "You haven't moved on because he has kept you hanging for so long. You should first decide whether you want him back in your life or not, then giving any length of time would make sense. Having hailed from such a conservative and orthodox family, I admire his courage but that doesn't mean you keep adjusting according to his will. It would be imbecilic on your part to give him another 4 months after having wasted 6 years of your life. So, if you are letting him in, then just tell him to rush."

"The course of true love never did run smooth." She was not going to live on another's terms, so she had to take the bull by the horns. The very next day, she texted him saying that she was out of this mess and that she wanted him to move on too. She did not even wish him on his birthday, which fell a week after hers. She wanted to break his expectations and do nothing that would please him. She was being imprudent for his own good, she later opined over a chat with him. She had cold feet but didn't want to take a chance on her dreams and aspirations. On the other hand, she really loved him so she made the toughest choice in her life. Letting him go almost made her fall between the chairs, but that was the bravest thing to do at that time. He appealed to her to give him at least a week to settle everything; she was surprised to hear 4 months shortened to a week now. He was eager to have her but not as eager to wait until her PG was over.

But it didn't really stop here. Like they say, "Life is a roller coaster and relationships are a huge one passing down to turmoil." They met and spoke less often. He was getting the hang of split-ups by then. It was on their way back on the bike one day, knowing that she was going to meet him for the last time, that she hugged him as tightly as she used to. As she wore her heart on her sleeves, she expressed her love and he didn't mention a thing. After a while, he said, "I want you to look ahead in life and get married to someone else, if not me." He shifted his look from her in the mirror and at that moment, his eyes were teary. Tears kept rolling down his cheeks and she couldn't take her eyes off him. He didn't even hold her hands and kiss them, nor did he stop her from hugging him, which used to be his normal reaction under the circumstances where his expectations were not rightly met. Maybe he knew that this might be their last meeting. He just rode the bike silently after that. Later, when she got off, he did all that looking into her eyes.

She knew that sooner or later he would say I love you back, he would hold her hands and kiss them. He himself would not be able to resist. He may have sat down and bewailed later at his home, but wasn't successful in convincing her to change her mind. She acquainted him with her worries and insecurities related to her career. "You may have to wait if you really want me back. Also, I forgive you for everything, if that is why you became this serious," she conferred. Like they say, "Time heals all wounds," she wanted to recover from this heartbreak and look forward to her life, whereas he still wanted them to remain in touch for old time's sake to which she replied that he would object to his own desires once he was married. When push came to shove, he tapered his frequency of calls and messages by himself and she slowly came back to being normal.

Like the saying goes, "There is never clear sailing without a hitch," she fortuitously topped her batch in both semesters despite all the hurdles and stress. But somewhere in the middle of the 2nd semester, Dheeraj started calling her again. From their last conversation, she could recall him voicing his wish to settle in the Middle East. The construction business was more productive there and Civil Engineers got desirable remuneration as compared to India was what he had told her, explaining exactly why he wanted to be there. It was after a year and a half that he had called. She accepted his excuses this time, thinking he must have been busy handling itsy-bitsy legal customs in stages. She was aware of how the paperwork and follow-ups run in perpetuity. "It's a great deal of work and takes an ample amount of time to settle in a new country. It's different that you have remembered me after a long gap," she mentioned on the call.

She was anyway waiting to deliver the news of her new field in those days. And she had a lot of other things to spiel. It still shook her like a leaf watching his call appearing on her mobile screen, or maybe he got more willies than her. But they had always been slightly queasy when they talked. However, she was not as uncomfortable as usual whereas a wave of tension could be made out from his speech even today. They spoke till his balance was naught. Their relationship was coming to a turn because in a matter of days he waved at her on WhatsApp with an intention of **making confessions**; something he had bottled up for a cocoon's age and wanted to release. It was evening in Dubai but she had already hit the bed here. He began his confessions and kept her awake for a long time that night. He went on revealing about the girl he had bluffed about at one point when he was studying in College. He conceded that there was no such girl. He couldn't think of any name so a name that rhymed with her quickly came on his tongue. He never actually had any girlfriend. He wanted to express how he felt but there were many things going on in his life at that time. Little did he know that he would lose her because of that. She emphasized on questions about their inactions and faults.

She was too naive to pick his brain. She wished she had inquest the matter, she wished she had been smarter and more influencing, more extrovert and eloquent, she exclaimed. She was blaming herself the whole time for not being able to catch the clues. They were guilty of their own flaws and errors. He was guilty of his gaffes and blunders. She was remorseful for having missed the chance but she was no duck to water then as she was before. It was a night tide and she didn't want to remain in a sad sight for long. To let go of that situation she said, "Maybe this was all preordained; we were never destined to be together and that's our pitiless exorable fate. I am glad that our relationship has shaped up through these years. We can talk without any feelings of gauche and edginess, which happens while speaking to past lovers and that's only because we are friends today." He couldn't agree more and had to comfort himself with this only choice of seeking solace.

He didn't jump ship for another year. He kept her posted. Their chats became less frequent but were longer and they sprang everything about themselves in a nutshell. During this time, her other sister, Surekha, had moved in to live with them. She was pissed by their mum's constant pessimistic thoughts back home, a flaw ingrained in her mum didn't let her stay in peace with her ongoing preps for GATE. Now the house they were staying in was small and they somehow adjusted under the same roof. As fate would have it, the situation fell harder on them as they ran out of personal savings and none of them were working. With their business at home dropping in a heck overnight, they were financially unsteady. The landlord had given the whole house on lease because he needed a tidy sum for his daughter's marriage. With the area tenanted to students, it was next to impossible to find a small house of affordable rent. Ultimately, they had to rent a spacious house that was out of their budget, wherefore they had a real crunch by cutting down on various other things to make a living. Even though they were going through torrid times together, they still said, "Fortitude comes easy when you are assembled."

2018

They were living in turmoil for a few months, then everything got dispensed. It all happened like a bolt from the blue. Rekha scouted for information about events from her friends and volunteered as a promoter one day. The money she had made on the first day by simply pitching to facile work knocked her socks off. She then pulled Prema too into the game and they never really had to struggle for money after that as the field taught them easy ways to earn it. Prema made a modest start by getting into service work and they later dipped into corporate events as promoters. Further, her networking purveyed to films and she began appearing in small roles in advertisements and feature films. She continued doing this part-time on weekends to earn the extra money even after she started a paid internship for the role of a Copywriter in one of the ad agencies of good repute towards her 4th semester. She had laid her hands everywhere possible but she now wanted to make a lucrative career in writing. Anyway, it was a blessing in disguise that they got the idea about events when they needed help the most. They could even send home every extra penny that they saved.

Something awful yet interesting happened after shifting to this house. The frequency of Dheeraj's calls and messages increased. He would regularly visit her DP and status, and made it even more prominent by commenting on them. By this time, they had already formed a School WA group, so sometimes they would be engaged talking in the group and sometimes they shot the breeze personally. She was on a week-long tour to Hyderabad, where it all actually started. Now, she had set off for two things – one was to meet her same close friend, Ayesha, who lived in the city and the other was to return her uncle's misplaced headset, which slave to his old habit he had forgotten weeks ago when he visited them. The day she was heading to her uncle's house from her friend's place, Dheeraj happened to ping her on the way. Since it was a 5-hour journey, he could get her attention for a longer stretch. Even after reaching, they were awake and conversed until dawn.

He began talking about why he had sloped off for more than a year when they were both studying. This is when he made his **2nd confession.** He had held his horses for a long time and wanted to offload everything possible that night. He asserted that things had changed after his mother's demise. He turned into a severe drug addict and dabbled in heroin, marijuana, and charas. The smoke and drinks were no pleasure to get as high as kites, so he escaped to being stoned. The doses of these recreational drugs were so heavy that he ended up in the rehab center. This is why he couldn't express his love for her bluntly even after she had done several times on the call. Lost in his own world, he didn't even know what he was doing. He started with a beer and just about 2 sticks of cigarettes every day. That grew to some 40 sticks along 6 pegs within a month.

Later, when 6 pegs felt inadequate, he ventured into the world of drugs because he wanted higher forms of intoxication. He started off with ganja, then dabbled with magic mushrooms, heroine, and charas. Those days, one of his own lecturers was a dealer, supplying those illegal drugs to a chain of student users. There were days he puzzled over smoked cigarette buds. His need to quench a narcotic taste that left him feeling euphoric had rocketed. He became a hophead. In order to meet their extortionate prices, he gave tuitions, handled equipment at wedding events, and did what not. Then, he understood that he was already caught in this vicious circle and there was no going back. His body had lost control; drugs had altered the way his brain and body functioned. He ceased to enjoy anything for that matter. The only interest and focus that remained intact was his love for basketball. His olfactory sense diminished and everything tasted the same; his health had deteriorated awfully. As a result, he landed up having backlogs in College.

When he tried to cut down on them, his body reacted appallingly and he became sick. His body was exhibiting withdrawal symptoms due to a sudden drop in taking opioids, which they were once used to. Neither could he inform his family nor did he have any girlfriend to seek help from. On top of all that, he had lost touch with her. Even he was dying to bounce back to his normal life. To his sheer luck, he had a set of friends who turned helpful. The problem with him was that after 5 PM in the evening, he developed that strong urge to consume drugs. So, they cuffed him in a chair and left him all alone in the room. He was so restless that he could do anything to fetch those drugs. He needed some or the other thing to intoxicate him, that was his condition. An hour had passed and his throat was drying up. No one showed upon purpose and even when they came to cross-check, they bolted the room after watching him freak out and beg to be set free. He did try to untie himself and in that attempt, toppled from the chair. This exercise continued for 3 to 4 days. On the 4th day, he vomited blood and the substance. Blocking the endorphins had caused these painful symptoms to occur because the same endorphin had earlier bound with the neuron receptors releasing high-levels of dopamine, which were responsible for giving him a high. Now the high was more intense than anything experienced during sex or an exceptional meal.

The underlying fact is that humans cannot control the release of endorphins other than through opioids. The brain cannot distinguish between opioids and the natural chemical produced, which is why the concentrated potency of the drug would feel overwhelming at first. The drug attaches to the receptors in the brain and changes the way the body sends and receives messages about pain and pleasure. When the body doesn't know what it is experiencing, it tends to get rid of that unexpected substance. This happens even when one is consuming them. The effect of the drug kicks in and the mind begins to experience euphoria when one is done vomiting. All opioids fight pain very naturally and the tolerance to that builds up so people need more of such drugs to feel substantial relief and extreme highs. When regular users stop using them, their bodies feel pain. Later, the brain begins to crave the feeling associated with its use. What's frightening is the addictive quality; while the brain still develops tolerance, the body does not. It slows down the respiratory system. When the dose is too big, our CNS and RS may become so overwhelming that they shut down. People become sleepy and they can even stop breathing due to hypoxia and high levels of carbon dioxide.

His friends rushed him to the nearby hospital after they witnessed such barfs with blood and black substance. The

Doctor noticed the marks of the ropes on his wrists and legs, and perhaps understood the situation. Dheeraj took a little time to explain his determination to overcome the addiction, listening to which the Doctor referred him to one of the rehab centres. He was allotted a room there, which was quite neat and clean. There were a few yoga books too on the table. The first night, Guru Ji came to his room and handed him a peg of whisky, telling him that quitting at once was not a good idea and that his body needed it right now. He quaffed it in a second and asked for another. Guru Ji politely refused and despite that, he bristled at his deplore. When Guru Ji placated him with his soothing words of wisdom, Dheeraj was brought to his sense of cool. He had been an insomniac for many days but slept soundly that night. They woke up every morning at 5AM and the day commenced with yoga sessions, particularly meditation.

Guru Ji explained that everything was born from our mind, so it needed to be efficiently trained to attain control. They were served breakfast at 9AM and 1 hour in the afternoon was reserved for interaction sessions with the residents. The meals consisted of only vegetarian food. This was where he turned into a total vegetarian. Evening meals were purposely kept light so that their attention went to satiating their hunger rather than in any forceful thought of intoxicating themselves. They had 3 prayer sessions every day. There were play areas where they could indulge in a few indoor games if they wanted. No source of distractions was entertained, neither newspapers nor visitors. His cell phone had already been deposited at the counter before he was let in. They were not supposed to have any contact with the outside world until the treatment was over. They lived a routine life that aided in keeping themselves disciplined in some way. During his course of interaction with the residents, he realized his problems were nothing compared to theirs.

Whisky was served for the first 5 days in a tapering quantity. On the 6th day, wine was served in place of whisky. His craze in terms of addiction had spiralled far down. Dheeraj's behaviour was getting a lot better by acclimating to this simple and healthy lifestyle. He had 17 backlogs in the 4th year, and by this time all of his batchmates were already placed in various jobs. He had missed enough classes to be detained, so in 6 weeks, he went with his concern to Guru Ji, requesting him to let him go. Though Guru Ji was convinced, he still wanted him there for 2 weeks more. In 8 weeks, Guru Ji himself released him. On the last day, he was given permission to do anything he wanted. To be fair, he just wanted to self-evaluate as to how he would want to take himself forward. He was planning his life's boat that day, so except for having food, he did not come out of his room. Sometime in the evening, Guru Ji came to his room like the first day and asked him for Guru Dakshina. He felt already in debt for his new life. When he asked what he could give him, Guru Ji had him take an oath that hereafter he would always help people who were suffering like him. No one in this world had benefited from such an act that he possessed. Not only was he enlightened but was equally appreciated for his cooperation. Lastly, Guru Ji mentioned that nothing would have been possible without his will, so he counted this as their success together.

It seemed that he had missed her to an extent that he had turned to writing poems for her in his spare time. He had decided that once he cleared all his backlogs and was well-settled with a nice job, he would call and confess everything. However, by the time things settled and he approached her, it was already late. She was committed by then.

She had the drift of his condition; she had seen addictions at home. Her father had been stewed for maximum time before he passed away. She had been exposed to such intoxicated people wherever she went, even in her neighbourhood at Aizawl. It was there to be seen all over Aizawl for us. We got to spot drug addicts, and especially at night, had to walk through them. Maybe she was dewy and not very quaint on the phone, otherwise she was self-aware, privy to people and situations to her naked eye. She had been brand new to this city then, just like an immaculate suit. Maybe that's why she failed to identify such drastic changes in him while they were talking. If she had, she would surely have handled it differently, in fact, they would have been together now, she evinced. She couldn't almighty wish any less even then. It was almost morning by the time this conversation sort of ended.

He called her up the next day to make sure that she had reached back to Bangalore safely. He also divulged his plans of visiting her that year, on his way to Kerala. He called her again in a few weeks, concerned about her illness. The symptoms of tonsillitis had really knocked her out for a six, and she couldn't speak due to the agonizing pain in her throat. He called the moment she was on the mend and ready to talk. Soon the call intervals lessened and chats mounted up. They technically had an update from morning to night, where they exchanged their hearts and minds. They really enjoyed their conversations and he never made any attempts to conceal his feelings of intrigue towards her anymore. He would comment on her status or display pictures on his own. He would tell her overtly what he felt about her sex appeal, how he found her better now after she putted on some weight rather than being skinny. How he was crazy about her long hair, and how he found her pouted lips tempting. He never felt objected to her clothing, and in turn, liked her being upgraded and spiffy. He liked her fad approach and confidence in carrying herself. He found her presentation elegant and nifty, put her personality on a pedestal, and such things.

Later one day, he made his **3rd confession**. Now, he didn't want to hold himself from saying those 3 words to her. He wanted to release himself from the thought that he could never tell her. He started off by sending her one of those romantic poetries that he had written in her memory when he was in the rehab, and subsequently vented out, "I had a job, I was in my right frame of mind, and clean enough to start a family. That's why I felt that the time was most suitable to propose. It was with this perspective and motive that I had messaged you in 2011. I was about to confess when you opened up about your commitment to your ex-boyfriend, Faiz. You even began asking about my made-up girlfriend, which was a mooted question by then. **I regret all the time I wasted without expressing myself clearly. I regret that I couldn't marry you.** I welcome any change in you whole heartedly. I loved you even when you were skinny because you mattered to me as a person utmost. I love you and I am proud of how you have evolved." He sent her pictures that he had somewhere archived to substantiate his statement. She was taken aback to find out how he had saved her old pictures. Even she didn't have some of them as she had already removed them from her FB account. His love was unostentatious and placid, and that's why he called himself an obsessed lover. She was his first and was going to be his last love as well, whereas in her case, he was not her last.

She had left him far behind and didn't have the nerve to accept that she still loved him. She had accepted their fate long ago and could assuage him with the same. She didn't love him was also what she had replied to counter-interact. He continued to call her up anyway. In the following days, he asked her out for rides as they were both crazy about road travel. He expounded that he would sponsor a trip when he came to Bangalore. He would get his car and they could travel by road. Somehow, he wanted to make their meeting memorable. She noticed him being very enthusiastic and determined in the way he charted that tour so intricately. She was already impressed. Coorg was his final plan, and he was arriving a week before his birthday. There was a transport of delight and profound joy to behold for both of them. They were counting the months and days, especially her, because she had prepared a 13 by 14 sized family frame to gift him in advance when she would meet him. It had a beautiful collage of pictures of him with his wife and children, and she hoped that he would like it to an extent that he wept with joy.

However, she stood wearing a thick shell whenever he would emote his feelings irresistibly. But she began entertaining his hugs and kisses emojis and GIFs at night before they fell asleep. She was really enjoying the care and attention showered upon her, and more than that, being loved by him. Though they invoked a canoodle sensation in her, she kept herself on the receiving end. She tried to shield her sentiments for a long time. He fessed up saying that he had pledged his trot and in spite has never been faithful to his wife because she lingered deep in his thoughts and mind always. She was someone he had loved from School and it wouldn't go away, whatever done. But he was used to this double life now. Neither of them could actually take away their presence from deep within their minds and that was the truth. As days were descending, his feelings were getting ambivalent. He was elated and brittle, due to which he would have made some 10 changes in the oncoming trip. He was just chopping and changing them. At one point, he even started thinking about situations like what if he kissed her soon after hugging her in excitement when they met. A hug might happen very spontaneously and he can kiss her on the cheeks, were her words of assurance. Later, he mentioned that he was seeking permission for kissing her on her lips. That just left her grinning ear to ear. She was over the moon and also tongue-tied. She had fantasized about making love with him in endless ways before, even then she didn't want to cross the line to a proper affair.

She was straddling on the fence so she bit her tongue and responded in a diplomatic way. She asserted, "If you have any galls to kiss me like that in public then you may." She didn't doubt his courage at that point but that was her wittiest way of waking his instinct. She let her head rule her heart. Within a few days, he came back into his former state of mind. He was on the guilt trip and contrite that he had got his motor revving and everything he said had been in the heat of the moment. He sought her forgiveness and swore that he would do nothing disgraceful when they meet. As they were coming close to that day, she was in 7th heaven. She was going to meet him after 12 long years, so she was happy to flee the whole time without realizing the trouble that was brewing already. It was difficult to just calm down and really wait, but when the rain pours, it pours.

He had plans of venturing into a business in Kerala in the upcoming years and had returned home for that reason.

He had sent his wife and kids back a few months ago because he wanted them to settle down and have a steady, formal education in one place. He was supposed to leave for Bangalore as per the plan, once he was done with his cardinal work. Since she had no update after he reached his state, she rang him twice to check on his status. He didn't answer but she wasn't fretful and distraught until he explained everything the next day himself. "I am cancelling the trip and wouldn't be able to make it," he wrote straight away on WA. He was conveying in bits and pieces even when she asked him what happened. She was initially annoyed, then told him to cut the chase and tell her the real matter. She had to force him to unveil the complete truth. "My wife has happened to read our last conversations after I missed covering my tracks. From that moment, she has locked herself in the bedroom and gone hush. Even now, I am drinking at my farm house in Palakkad. Our likelihood of divorce is devastating the family, so I am high-strung and stressed. That's why I am even thinking of heading back to Dubai tomorrow," he evinced. The whole thing made her feel guilt-ridden and she sent him the picture of that frame to cascade his wife's misunderstanding. Then she not only advised him to cancel the trip but even insisted that he bring his wife and kids along to Bangalore. "I will just show up to hand over the frame. You all could spend the rest of your time exploring the city. Seeing this, her insecurities might eradicate without any effort," she exhorted.

But he had no intention of correcting the situation while she was after resolving it. He was drowning in danger and all he could think of was an escape. Silvi was affable at the moment, so there was no use beating around a dead horse was what he wheeled out. She asserted, "You are going to create a very wrong impression of our relationship if you don't lift your spirits and care to clear Silvi's doubts." They never had cross swords in their lives as they did in those 2 days. The next day, he recommended trashing the frame like a reckless and insolent being. His repulsive behaviour indicated that her respect was of little account. There was no spark of decency as she had expected from him in such crucial times. He had even left the School WA group in anger. She didn't want him to disconnect from their friends because of her, so she continued adding him in the group every time he exited. I am not sure if anyone in the group had noticed the melodrama since no one really stood up and asked. He could easily block Prema but he wasn't doing that. She hung her head in embarrassment, felt chagrined and disgraceful of him. She was completely bumped out.

AFTER PG

Bangalore

She had it up to here and was no longer interested in building the bridge. It was a matter of her self-respect too. Her seething resentment came to a boiling point and she declared that she was cutting their friendship off. She wept and started effing, "You will never have a daughter for having disrespected me so ruthlessly." Having a daughter was one of his pining desires and he had once imparted that he and Silvi were planning a 3rd baby. She couldn't believe that he could be so dodgy, she didn't believe him at all now and subtly hinted the same. Her same close friend from Hyderabad, Ayesha, had come over to the city for a few days after that incident. Just when she was busy strolling around shopping with her, Dheeraj casually messaged her that he was still in Kerala. In case she was willing to change her mind, he would come alone to meet her as decided. She was fuming with this negative vibe for many days. So, the next time he texted her, she straight away declined.

Later, her sister, Surekha was placed in VIT and went on to pursue her M.Tech in Chennai. This just nullified her recent ghastly past; like they say, "For those who wait,

God gives in abundance." The house was now big and expensive for just the two of them again, so they started scouting for another one. Her studies were nearly over and she had started a paid internship at this time. Post her internship, she continued working for the same advertising company as a Copywriter. The position was right up her alley and she joined. She killed two birds with one stone – got the internship certificate as well her job confirmed on a contract basis.

2019

A Copywriter's profile is considered higher and they are usually paid well per diem than Content Writers. However, in her case, she had a mere 9-month writing experience before that so was compensated accordingly. What lent deeper satisfaction was that her starting salary was way better than when she was a Nurse. She knew that Dheeraj was not at ease; 4 months had passed since that incident, so he was simply waving and enquiring about her well-being on WA. Now, she was not someone who was going to entertain his blather, hence she spoke to the point and bid his explanation. She exhorted him to speak the truth without fabricating even a little. She didn't want him to delude with any less truth, she stated brusquely. He fell on the sword and apologized for having hurt her erroneously. Then, he explained everything blow to blow.

It seemed that his wife had his phone while he was playing with the children at the beach around noon. He was to leave in the evening as planned. When she saw someone calling on his Dubai number, she began to investigate because he hadn't saved her number. He scooped the story, twisting the facts around a bit. Without referring to her name, he said it was a friend from Bangalore who had called. They had planned a get-together with schoolmates. Then she drilled further into the matter and asked him to show her the group chat. As he obviously didn't have any evidence of it, she unlocked his phone to verify. Their chat was open and she happened to read it all. He then had to face the music. No woman can stand her spouse holding feelings for someone else, but she was clever enough to be able to attack his mind. They were going no astray and having an affair the way she was thinking, but she was already condensed with her insecurities. Silvi wanted him to create a fuss, misbehave, and act rough enough to make sure she hated him forever. It was also her idea to make him leave the group. When Prema still didn't believe him, he became rebellious. His temper rose and he retorted in a snap that he didn't have anything left to say, whether or not she believed him. They didn't speak for more than a year properly after that incident. Maybe she was the cynical one but his ego did not once let him go after her to appease her anger or mollify the situation. His ego felt greater than her worth to him, as far as she could see. Anyway, she looked forward in her life to things that were still left to be done, the first being moving to another area.

In the meantime, Dheeraj had re-joined the group and was involved in chats and sending forwards. He was constantly active, trying to seek her attention. However, she never bothered to respond after being dishonoured that way. It was his fault; he couldn't fight for her pride in front of his wife. She felt they were his flaws and not his wife's to blame. Most of our batchmates were married by this time, and so was I. Madhavan had a 4-year-old daughter with the same woman he had once called to talk about. Our lovely bro, Suresh was hitched to his lady love, who he had met when the couple were giving job interviews together, initially, when they were in Bangalore. Above all that, her ex-boyfriend, Faiz had got spliced to someone arranged for him. This was the only year when he called on her birthday to wish her and then, they never spoke. The best part about relocating to this area for her was that she had found a music institute at a convenient distance where they taught violin.

Anyway, her terms in the current company were over and instead of taking a short term extension, she chose to resign. She had a short life there, otherwise she was planning to stay longer if she wasn't pulled into the dirty game of work politics that normally appears during the time of appraisals in corporations. She got an opportunity to work for more than a year before she winded up her impending projects. This sort of distorted her mind and well-being for some time, and then she thought it was time to be more lucid with herself. This was when she decided to take a break and went home. Further, she reduced the frequency of events and focussed on searching for job alongside her other activities.

In due course, her sister who was studying at VIT, received a letter of internship from ISRO, which was a long walk of half an hour from their home. Once again, the house became small for all of them together. Fortunately, this time they had a good option of another house, which belonged to the same landlord, so they moved in there without having to budge anywhere too far. It was a few yards away from where they lived, and also close to the metro station and technically, ISRO. It was her dream to live with her siblings once in her life again, so it felt like a tiny whim coming true. As they say, "He who has no sisters looks with some degree of innocent envy on those who may be said to be born to friends." She counted this bond to be as important as that of a husband and wife, because they are the only people who know what it's like to have been brought up the way you were. One of her sisters, Rekha, had picked up another job, which was not relevant to the media industry, but her life was spinning a yarn. Her schedule was on the same roll, hectic with job interviews and other activities. It took her more than a year this time to find another job in the field of copy/content writing.

2020

She got her head around the job search and addressed herself in a number of interviews even this year. She was racking her brain with writing assignments when at home. She even pushed her luck by writing screenplays for competitions. But she began to minimize doing events furthermore. She thought that once she got her feet under the table, she would rule out how to make more time for her other interests. Essentially, she was working all the hours God had sent her. She had plans to call out to her friends only after she hacked a job, until then she wanted the champagne to remain on the ice, and that's why she had no real feelings for it even on her birthday. However, she didn't want to ruin the happiness that her siblings sought in arranging things for her, so she stayed in good spirits for their sake. She was genuinely in heaven,watching them glorify her birthday.

Now, Dheeraj had happened to wish her on the group to seek her attention. He had no other way to say that he thought of her all the time. She replied to his courteous wishes out of chivalry; this is one incident that proves women can also retain that sense towards men. Nothing except those wishes and regards came up afterward. This time around, life came to her as a completely different surprise and a highly unanticipated change. The terrible disease of Covid-19 called for disaster in a span of a few days and changed her life for another 1 year. She had scraped through the job and had 2 offer letters lying in her mail. At the same time, one of her sisters, Surekha, had received a joining letter as a contract employee following an internship from ISRO, plus 2 weeks of holidays were declared for interns and temporary staff. She was full of the joys of spring in a double treat and had already booked the ticket for going home, but nothing settled as to how it seemed because of the sudden outbreak of this contagious disease. The inevitable problems that the disease was letting cast a shadow over everything else, like when fat hits the fire. It put both of their careers on the backseat for long and they were crestfallen.

Cases were showing no signs of dropping, a lockdown had already been announced by the PM to check the spread of the virus, because breaking transmission was the only way to defeat the deadly coronavirus. Many died in extremity, whereas many recovered and the whole world was facing it. Every laboratory was working tight in finding a cure and ways of treatment. The medical and para-medical teams had to rack their brains for the next many months to find a solution. So, it was much like servicing in the times of war. I heard that after the black disease in 1999, it was Covid that had become a pandemic to this extent. Treatment costs were huge and the price of the medical kits was revised, which again was a different ball game of business. Because of the lengthy timeframe of the lockdown in obligation, it shook the economy badly and that suddenly turned the whole world upside down. Some businesses were picking up and many had to excessively cut down their costs, thus taking away people's employment from all walks of life. The growing instability in the economy was not letting any private hands or indentured servants feel secure. It rigorously destroyed everything at once.

The news channel was flooded with corona news every day; the virus was circling like a vulture, and it felt worse than the 1990s tsunami. The pandemic was creating history because the cases were prevalent in China, and were known to have occurred in a place named Wuhan. The country was striking wealthy profits through apps even in such times amongst which tik tok had the largest users, ranking in most dibs. Our government decided to ban all their apps in order to report the gravity of the situation and what mistakes had landed them here. This severe action had already been taken by other countries slightly in advance. Scientists were inventing preventive vaccines, which were running on trials. Free Covid tests were sponsored in most contaminated zones. The contribution of our health team was anecdote at different times through lighting lamps at night and drumming utensils-like activities. This action was to mark the unity of the Nation in enhancing moral support to help them combat the cases.

Like every coin has two sides, the situation was doing innumerable good by allowing people to spend quality time with their families, making time for things that could not be done earlier, and getting more gen on indoor exercises. People were turning to their old hobbies and some were able to nurture their creativity. They were using a portion of their time in connecting with old friends or in doing things they weren't able to heretofore think. At the same time, there was less pollution on the road, plants could take a good breath, and animals were liberated to walk free. People were learning a new art of living and the virus had associated them with newer medical terms and ailments. Also, I could see people being more careful and conscious than ever before.

Dheeraj was doing the same thing in his free hours; he was drawing sketches and sending them on the group. His crafts had always been indicative and impressive yet she managed to resist by not responding to them. A week after, he dropped her a text expressing his concern and regards for her and her family. Maybe he was looking to reconcile in a way, but she left unheeded in wrath. What kept her going in those days, when she was not doing any work-related assignments, was her music practice. As they say, "Music has the divine power of tranquillity, it would let your energy transform into an inquisitive mind."

But like a friend turns foe in bad times, her neighbour flipped out while she was practicing with her window open. She had heard the same neighbour bleating about the lockdown earlier in the evening, and after some time, he started yelling at her. When she went to her window to speak to him, he was pointing his finger towards her like an uncivilized and lippy person. He began threatening her about making a police complaint and was speaking in a brash tone throughout. It didn't seem as if he was agitated because she had disturbed him during his cat nap; he could quietly sleep in his bedroom if he wanted any silence. He was looking to pour out his frustrations and unfortunately, she became the victim of his ill temper.

His windows actually faced the people living downstairs; their family had a small girl-child and the house was never at rest. People in his own building made all sorts of noises till midnight, but he never upbraided amid their babbles. It actually hurt his ego when she didn't stop playing. He even called up her landlord to complain. He was bossy and shameless, behaving as if the lockdown was meant only for him and he owned the whole locality for that matter.

Like a barking dog never bites, she knew he wouldn't do anything beyond that, so she told him to do whatever pleased him. One of her sisters, Rekha, was petrified even after she told her that she would handle everything if he did lodge a complaint against her. She never really expected moral support from her, but Rekha was someone who always preferred to escape from any unpleasant situation. She moved to her boyfriend's place with the necessary stuff for a few days. From the next day, they were not in talking terms until she came back. Prema was piling in agony, it so upset her that she sat outside the temple in her lane, a place that always made her feel in high spirits and revived her whenever she was low. She went and slouched over movies; it was another thing that made her feel good in such times. Then she thought, why should she let that man spike her guns? What matters is her inner contentment in life, so a week later, she resumed her practice in the hall, latching every exit to avoid causing any disturbance to such people. In some days, her violin started making some unpleasant and awkward sounds as the sound post inside had got slightly displaced. The sound post is what transfers sound from the top to the back plate, altering the tone by changing vibrations. Nothing as yet had come out into the wash with the situations of covid-19. There was no way she could take the instrument anywhere to get it fixed, so she decided to reply to Dheeraj.

He was insanely crossing her mind at that point, and their friendship was poorly stained though he was always looking for ways to make up for the past. She never thought that she would turn around, but she did, and asserted that she would only proceed with the conversation after a proper explanation that he owed from last time. She left the ball in his court, but really had to pull herself together before messaging him. She began by replying to his previous questions, where he had asked about herself and her family. He must have been awake, which is why he promptly came online. There was no change in his explanation till the point when he had said that he was caught dead. He said that everything started from the moment she rang him to confirm whether he had started his journey to Bangalore. When his wife began to investigate, he tried escaping by simply lying about the reunion. He even sent her the pictures taken on that afternoon with the date and time encircled. Then he said that his wife wished to see the group chat; as her doubt had solidified when he didn't have any conversation regarding planning a reunion. That made her immediately unlock his phone and their chats were lying right there, open. He had forgotten to erase their previous day's conversation when he had even expressed his love for her. Due to his wife's nescience of the English language, he managed to twist the facts and convinced Silvi that it was nothing like what she was thinking. Somehow, he took the rap for everything that day.

He went on to tell her that there had been many other incidents where Silvi had suspected him of having affairs with every female that he interacted with, and this started not long after their marriage. She was extremely possessive and insecure because somewhere she felt inferior and not up to the mark for him. She had even accused him of having affairs with his students, in the early days of their marriage. She would keep prying into his phone when he was around for her own satisfaction. She pushed his button when she accused him of having an affair with his late mother; it had reached that point of culmination where he couldn't help himself from slapping her tight that day, he vented.

Prema held her in disfavour from when she had seen their wedding pictures on Facebook. His wife seemed like one cunning fox the way she had ruled over him. Even we never believed their shotgun situational marriage story in the first place. It was a hard truth to swallow. Even then, she didn't want to be biased; she had a feeling that his wife's doubts would have sourced from something relevant in the past, the way Dheeraj still kept up to his taciturnity with her. But this time she gave him a choice to lay bare his affairs even if he had any without any second thought. She was trying to take him into confidence, assuring him that he could confide all his worries to her. She wanted him to be unreservedly truthful and for that, she had to win his dreadful trust. She went on repeating the questions at least twice in case he was hiding his claws and pretending to be nice.

"As a woman, you may be a bit inclined towards my wife, but men aren't always the culprits, Prema. I've never had any extramarital affair," he riposted. He was amplifying his statements by saying that he knew he had been the kiss of death but was obligated to follow his wife's commands. Silvi didn't like her since the day she heard that she was his ex-girlfriend. He was putting all the cards on the table now, and Prema realized that there was no love lost. Subsequently, he forwarded the screenshot of her previous profile picture on Facebook with his comment below. He caused her to remember that moment to explain when it all started. Prema was wearing a short red dress in the picture to which he had commented 'nice legs'. His wife had rubber-necked and seen that compliment. Then, Silvi had heedfully asked, "Why only legs?" Now, for someone like us, because of the place we are rooted in, we consider such remark bog standard. We are used to seeing ladies in bolder outfits back in Mizoram. Therefore, she found his comment quite normal. There was nothing that she had minded but his wife's scrutiny went further and she poured over her Facebook profile. When Silvi learnt that both of them hailed from the same place, she called his younger brother, Surya, to investigate.

Their topic had been running around the house from our School days and they often teased him with her. She was the talk of his house from the day she had handed him the gifts and met his elder brother. His younger brothers casually called her his girlfriend ever since. Now, his brothers Surya and Prakash were not aware of his wife's basic nature and her intention behind calling them all of a sudden. They were in hysterics when Silvi called and uttered Prema's name, so they happened to tell her that she was Dheeraj's ex-girlfriend. His wife did not quite follow the joke that was passed on to her that instant, which was obvious. They realized their colossal mistake when Dheeraj enjoined not to kid around with his wife anymore. They happened to process Silvi's cultured doubt into hatred at that very moment by digging the hole. They had unknowingly screwed everything up. Then his wife not only made him exit the School WA group but also forced him to delete Prema's number and warned him to stay away from her. This is why he couldn't save her number post hoc. He had by-hearted her number thereon. He felt strangulated, like he was married to a ball and chain. This feeling had later on induced him to cook up the divorce story, which he would have done if they did not have any children.

He was talking to her despite his wife's angry remonstrance because he was that tortured and lonely and felt like venting out his long-hidden feelings for her. Come rain or shine, he thought he would confess this time and so he did 2 years ago. Then, he requested her to analyse the situation from his standpoint and at last apologized for having hurt her badly. She responded back the same afternoon and asked him to figure out his wife's mental status. His wife didn't seem to be playing in her full deck and there was no cure for doubts in this world, she opined. He had felt the need himself after observing Silvi's consistently irrational behaviour and happened to speak about psychiatric counselling. She got so offended that she created a scene right then and there. She got the wrong end of the stick and perceived his approach as though he was thinking of her as an insane case. Her pugnacious attitude did not let her cooperate with him. She liked to call the shots all the time, so his opinion made no difference to her. He never had the guts to ask her again, he expressed.

He also asserted that they shared no common interests; she wouldn't encourage pursuing his interests alongside the job. They would always have their wires crossed because their trains of thoughts were different. She wouldn't even give him any privacy when he wanted to be all by himself watching sports on TV, playing games, reading books, or just sketching. As a man, he could be shooting hoops with his friends, catching a flick with some others, flapping with friends on chat or call. But she couldn't stand to have his attention away from her. For instance, if he was hooting at the cricket score, she would smirk and wrinkle her nose in the kitchen. If he enjoyed something on his own, she felt side-lined, which is why he gave reins to those activities only when she and the children were away. But the thing was that whenever he was not around, he had to update his schedule, send a screenshot of whoever he was talking to, especially when he was online for late hours. She rubbed his nose in all the wrong ways like that. Whereas with him, he never checked her phone as he trusted her despite her past mistakes. He had bitten off fulfilling his responsibilities as a husband and father. He didn't let her stay a grass widow for long. He never abandoned her, but she wouldn't understand and respect him the way he expected her to. What hurts him most was the way she treated him in return. They had stormy relations from the start. But if he had been aware of all these even a bit earlier, he would not have taken the risk of marrying her in any case. He is badly fucked up in his marriage and he would have to accept his fate now, he reflected with sadness on his unhappy married life.

This conversation was happening when he was stuck in Dubai for 2 weeks after demission due to the circumstances. His flight was on hold and he was waiting for the airline openings and the official permission to travel on his credentials. He had plans of returning to India. Prema was busy with the nuts and bolts of her schedule, racing against time. She would run around doing many things from dawn to dusk, even then she made time for him. She preferred talking less in the daytime and more at night before going to bed. He did limit his messages according to her convenience and availability but also mentioned that after going back to his family in Kerala, he would be restrained to message her the way he was able to so freely in his wife's absence now. So, he wanted to make good use of this opportunity to be with her the most. Even after reading such messages, she thought of biding her presence by keeping her feelings for him neutral. It was the golden period of her life, which even she didn't want to miss. He had booked a flight for the 28th of April, so technically, she had about 8 days to be with him.

He was more or less harping on the same matter throughout those days. By then she had recognized that he was in a can of worms. So, she felt she could at best offer her company and some counselling from a distance. A bad marriage can feel like chains attached to the legs, so he would have to quit beating head against the wall. He would have to rule out his peace within this marriage, if he was in no position to leave Silvi due to their children. He must consider a psychiatrist, but before that he needed to start picking holes in her inadequate behaviour, so that he could prove her mental ailments and convince her to visit the Doctor. He should not neglect her sick mind because she could be in serious trouble too. Also, he had coddled her way too much, it was time he let her shoulder the responsibilities of earning and helping the family as well. He would have to be proactive and work assiduously to hammer out his action plans, she wrote.

The next moment, he was curious to know about her marriage plans. She was in the middle of work and it would have taken her a long time to wind up if she continued speaking, so she insisted he go to sleep. It was late at night but he was ready to wait for her answers. He was keen and all ears. Initially, she behaved impishly. Like curiosity kills a cat, she asked him back in jest why he was interested? He wouldn't advise anyone in this life to marry after his experience, worse than a bumpy ride, he replied. He was still waiting to receive one convincing answer, she noticed. Afterwards she replied,"I haven't created any legacy for someone to look after nor am I insecure or dependent, so being in love can be the only right reason to marry, it's not a very big deal for me otherwise. Besides, it's a huge responsibility and change for which I'm not ready yet; when it has to happen, it will happen," she finally replied. For some reason, he was trying to seek more information about her desires and plans with a fine tooth comb. Since they went back a long way, he knew she never gave mediocre answers; she was decisive and not easily influenced. She made her own way and was very picky with people. He was moved by those shades akin in her. Their conversation was only about her that night. She would feel too self-centred anyway if she had done it on her own.

He was somehow flattered with her. She had enormous patience with him in spite of him being a rarely good listener and a trouble seeker, and this had helped develop more interest and respect towards her. He wanted to know her like the palm of his hand. Finally, she opened up about her plans of staying with her mother, whether or not she joined wedlock. Though he appreciated this idea rather than getting entangled in society's norms, he still underlined the importance of having a partner. He also expressed how unsatisfied he was for not being able to repay his own mother and also that he didn't want her to be left alone after her mum was no more. There was no shadow of doubt that she understood him the most. She genuinely and selflessly cared for him but now he was showcasing how much he cared for her. Well, what turned her down immediately was him cutting her short by asking if she had another messaging app installed, which his wife would be unaware of. Silvi was always ready for fights and if she found him online for this long and such late hours, she would crack the jackpot. He just wanted to avoid the blazing row. He didn't want to add insult to his injury, he stated.

Though she informed him instantly about having a telegram app in her phone, his query did not give her a very nice feeling. What made her continue talking was him trying to hark back to School days when he was around her. Those were the only 2 years they saw each other in the midst of everything. So, she let him continue his talks of adulation even when he asked if he should leave it for later and allow her to sleep. He was talking highly of her. She never knew till that day that she had captured his attention to that level. She was always in his eyes. She was sort of enjoying, knowing, how he liked to keep a tab on her. That proclaimed his love and interest towards her. So, she started riding herd on him, such that she insisted he disclose everything about her from that time. She had been killing his pleasure of keeping secrets; he said she was his secret love but it did not bother her at all. She made him expose about all her puerile behaviour that had vote for his change of heart.

They were brushing up their old memories. Suddenly he dropped a bombshell which literally tickled her to death; she never knew that he had taken up Hindi language because of her. This way, he made his **4**th **confession** to her, stating that he really had to struggle learning it. He would stick to the last bench from where it was easy to sneak around and no one would notice. He never even allowed anyone to sit next to him and spoil the pleasure of watching her without any distraction. His family flew off the handle for him having dropped Biology without consulting them. They were not in approval of it. In fact, they forced him to study Science when he was good at Arts. He fell off to Engineering quite unlettered at that time, like she fell into Nursing once inspite of being equally good in Arts. **He still regretted not taking Arts and making conscious choices in his career.** Dropping Biology was no big loss as he was on the road to Engineering. But he could at least saved himself from the blast that he took for her, she said. He didn't want to lose the chance of watching her closely, so picking Hindi was his act of boldness, he explained.

This brought her to asking him how his love was so consistent and what drew his attention initially? He said he liked her hair from the start and the tint of brown added to its craze. He found her beautiful, and in addition, her qualities appealed to him more. He found her smarter than her age, smarter than anyone in the Non-Mizo group. She hadn't taken Math, wasn't after Engineering or under the pressure of impressing people, which significantly proved her attitude of being absolutely carefree and decisive. She wasn't as introverted as he was though she spoke less. She had the confidence to approach him and admit that she was in love with him in front of anyone. She never gave up on him despite anything. He took a shine to those qualities of hers. She did slay him, he evinced. When everyone was crying for her dad inconsolable, she was in defiance. Because she was silent and down to despair, for once, he thought she was pretending to be strong being the eldest. Maybe she didn't display her tears in public, she would have shed them alone later, he thought and that earned more respect for her, he asserted.

She explained that she was in the stage of denial when everyone else was mourning and that's why she couldn't ululate like them. Her woeful expression was the baleful influence of his father's death. She edified him by saying that those were the signs of her weakness instead. She recounted the whole incident when she had gone to meet the principal to request him to allow her to repeat the 2nd PUC. He was not aware of all that had happened after the board results as he had left for Kerala long before that. But he adored how she took the principal's reprobation as a challenge and cleared her board without sitting in the class. She never knew that she was being watched like a hawk before she even noticed him. He said he used to pray that she developed feelings for him since he had fallen head over heels for her already. He saw her on the first day of School when she came for admission with her aunt, and from that day on, she never left his mind. He sat for hours preening her gift of a birthday card and listening to 'Pehla Nasha' on his walkman in the bathroom. They were the after effects of her gifts. He loved her in all aspects, even today, he expressed.

She wanted to know if he was aware that even she used to watch him. He had been notified but never had the guts to look back, he was afraid he would blush. He wondered how she couldn't be aware of his feelings when he had made it so obvious by simply accepting her rose. He actually didn't know what the colour red indicated; it was Anup again who gave him that info. Anup was concerned about the fact that he had accepted the rose. Though they were neighbours, they became friends in MICE. Anup had kept him in dark for 2 years, because he realized that his close friend was gay only when they were together in Kerala during a crash course before Engineering. Anup seized the opportunity while everything was good and tried to come close to him. Anup grabbed him from the back when he was standing alone. He felt absurd and jolted him away. He didn't have the slightest idea that something like that could happen to him due to his lack of knowledge. No one in his friends' circle mooted about sex. He also shared an incident where he wasn't even penny wise and was pound foolish. They were travelling somewhere by bus after School when Anup came forward and suddenly kissed him on his lips. Though he felt uneasy and awkward even at that moment yet he couldn't smell the rat. It did hit him but he could not wildly guess that Anup could be swinging both ways. It was then that he discerned why Anup pre-empted him from having an affair with her. He had plans for himself, but his interest and concern were different from what he had projected those days. He was jealous and insecure in real life, so from that day onwards he clammed up with him, he explained. She was laughing till her stomach ached when he spilled this secret about them. She couldn't believe that Anup could be that obsessed with men nor could I, from how we had seen him flirting with girls. His body language was feminine but his interest could be male oriented, we thought.

Anup had spread the rumour that he had denied his feelings for her and kept saying, "They are only from her end." She asked if that was true. He confessed that he had denied it to bhaiya but hadn't revealed his feelings to anyone else. Bhaiya was an extrovert and had several girlfriends, yet he was hesitant to speak about her. He was an introvert plus was compared to bhaiya at home in reference to everything, so he could never develop a friendly attitude towards him and tell him openly about his feelings for her. Also, because they never had sisters, he didn't know how women functioned. He wished he had a sister he could take advice from. He was instead docile to Anup's dopes. He wished he had been smarter in approaching the right person for advice. He wished she had come forward and asked, then he wouldn't have denied. He had made up his mind that he was only going to tell her, but she never asked. By the time she had openly proposed, he was already an addict so he would beat around the bush whenever she expressed herself. He didn't know how to put forth his feelings, which was why he trumped up a story. He loved her but was scarred and shattered from within after his mum's demise. Lost in addiction, he didn't know what he was doing himself. She wasn't his priority; having said that, most people in his College still knew her as his girlfriend. He was popular among girls because he played basketball pretty well. It was when one of those girls from his batch proposed to him that he declared he was in a relationship with her.

He was not aware of her compartment results or the fact that she had repeated 2nd PUC, but he came to Aizawl looking for her during his 1st year vacation when they were not in touch. He had spotted a couple of our ex-classmates on the way and asked about her to everyone he met with cross purposes. He didn't want them to be inclined to think that she was his main interest and motive. But her good friend, Sneha, who was studying there in those days was jumping topics without giving any useful information about her and that's why he could not get any update regarding her. His father had settled in Kerala after retirement and she was here in Bangalore, so he never had any purpose of visiting the state again.

He wished he was less reserved and more outspoken. If he had made himself heard then things would have been different today. **He regretted that he couldn't express his feelings at that time.** He was in his optative mood that night. It negated a melancholic feeling in her whenever he spelled out his **regrets.**

The next day, he forwarded some pictures of the books he was reading. He was a voracious reader and could spend hours devouring books, but he hadn't read in almost 6 years, he sussed out. He felt that he had been too dedicated towards his family. Sometimes he thought about leaving everything and escaping somewhere. This marriage had shaken up his life. He got married in a haste and was repenting in leisure now. He wished he had never married. He wished he could cut loose from his mentally unstable wife and live in peace, he said dreamily. He was happy to tell her that in his wife's absence he was able to live a life he had missed. And in the middle of all this, she was someone who relieved his burden; like the saying goes, "Trouble sharing is halving the trouble."

She had been pink-slipped for many months now and her lifestyle had become sedentary due to the lockdown. She had lost the job even after receiving offer letters. Her responsibilities towards her family, the financial crisis, and expectations from her own self were haunting her day and night. She resonated with his feelings; somehow, they were on the same boat yet she had never shared her pain or conferred her problems until that day. They both had their own share of heavy crosses to bear and a blind can't lead another blind, so she preferred to keep her problems away from him. She too confided now how badly she wanted to escape to Ravi Shankar's ashram to attain peace and live a different life for sometime. So, she recommended he visit Isha yoga, especially because he was a follower of Sadhguru. "Copping out is not the solution and no one is in-charge of your happiness and inner peace. Your wife is least bothered and the children are small, so you must learn self-care and conceit, you must learn to fend for yourself. You can think of staying once for a week at least after you reach Kerala," she advised. They would both claw their way out someday, she assured him.

Her idea was to make him feel lighter in such a tense moment. He pointed out that the thought of his children wouldn't let him walk free any day. They were the ones he was living for. His second son had spelled out Apache before Amma. He mentioned the joy he felt when his son slept on his chest. In no time, she evinced that he could imagine lying down similarly on her chest right now. She was about to send him a hug GIF but she read the text saying, 'No! I don't want to commit the same mistake and embarrass myself. I don't want to pursue this kind of a chat,' so, she didn't send him one. However, she could chuff him immediately by saying that maybe he could caper alone in his room or at least imagine dancing with her. He thought his body was stiff, but would still give it a try if she is there to hold him, he exuberated.

The next day, he sent a comic draft for her to review. Not only did she come to understand about his love for stand-up comedy and dreams of opening a cafe, but also learned that Dheeraj was good enough in humour writing. He was trying to gather information about guitars, just the cost and how long it would take to learn the basics. Someone in his neighbourhood back in Aizawl was a guitar geek and he had always envied that. He was doing things that he had enlisted in his bucket once. He had already got the news from the airlines confirming that he could fly in a few days, so he was gathering the things he would need during his quarantine period. Somehow, he would have to get an Indian sim card once he reached Kerala, until then they could chat over messages, he expounded. She suggested 2 things, 1st – to not buy a guitar if it was going to just lie somewhere after a few days, and 2nd – to start considering opening a cafe and hiring an artist to perform with his script. He could extoll his flair for humour writing, which is the most difficult genre in writing. He had kept all the references in his script from Aizawl, which awakened their memories and they went on nattering about the place, its cuisines, his favourite chowmein coupled with soup and chutneys, and the culture of red tea with jaggery.

How he wanted to revisit his School, that restaurant where they gathered during School, and stroll around his house. How he wanted to reminisce about the glory days once again. He was expressing his wistful longing; if they could be together in the same city where it had all started.

The idea seemed super fascinating to her too, creating memories at the same place when they're older. But she didn't want to go back to a place where no destinies lay, which is why she had even chosen not to revert back to his idea of remaining in touch during quarantine. However, she would enjoy doing all the evil work by sending him pictures of the chowmein prepared in the exact native style to entice him. She took immense pleasure in teasing him.

This time he was very pissed when he began to text. His wife had fought tooth and nail with him in the day for staying online till late night, to which she always had an objection. Maybe this was why he got back to chatting on telegram. On the other hand, Prema had problems whenever he tried to play safe. She told him not to get goad into spoiling his mood and stab his happiness because of Silvi's gratuitous behaviour. There was no use in telling him anything to subdue his mind. He was very sensitive when it came to his wife and children. He would reiterate on the subject matter, she knew, which is why she tried to divert his mind by any means during such times. Those images she believed worked on soothing his mind, when deep down she had also realized that these were his tricks to continue talking over telegram.

He called her the night before he was boarding, and it was after 2 years they were hearing each other's voice. As expected, he spoke about his wife, how she was always after discovering him, how she intercepted his space and tried to literally find a world in him. Maybe he was done glossing over her defects, otherwise he had never whinged about her on call. However, they would always extenuate any serious matter by regaling it. Somehow the topic descended to his children and he opened up about his baby girl. Now her laughter dropped to the bottom a second after hearing that news like a curtain was raised to something she hadn't bargained for. She just went brain dead and mute while he continued talking to her. It took some time for her to congratulate him; she wasn't pretending to be happy entirely, just that she failed to hide her instinctive reaction.

Next, she was keen to find out when it had happened. It reminded her of the days when he was telling her that they were planning for their 3rd child, which she didn't really believe at that point in time, and then her curse words, when they last quarrelled. When she expressed what she was thinking and feeling, he didn't get offended. In fact, his tone was blithesome, maybe it worked the other way around was what he gaily blurted out. Sometime after this conversation, his balance became naught and the call got disconnected. He noticed her silence and the way she was apologetic for her words and expressed her remorse. He messaged her saying that he comprehended her state of mind and how ineptly and wretchedly he had hurt her then. So, he needed no explanation for that. Maybe some of his good karma would have let him receive a daughter like after years of austerity, he construed. Teertha was named after the same wait and patience. His daughter was the symbol of forbearance and perseverance.

He didn't delay a minute in sending Prema pictures of Teertha after they had lost connection. She was gazing at her pictures and weeping constantly. She had held herself stoic for many years, but that day she broke down. Those pictures cast her mind back to the olden days when she had dreamt of their marriage and a daughter.

She dredged up the same thing and elucidated how disheartened she was at the moment. She was wailing in **deep regret,** then settled down with the idea of gifting his daughter something. She was his flesh and blood and that was more than enough. He said that he would make sure she kept it throughout her life. The only issue out here was that he may not be able to reveal the source, but she had no problem keeping it anonymous. Nothing else mattered as long as it reached the right person, she said explicitly. He was taken aback to see this side of her, extremely vulnerable, so he put a feeler to ascertain his importance. He asked her something that she hadn't ever asked herself. He was making her pick between him and Faiz. She asserted that both are special in their own ways, so she'd rather not pick any.

If truth be told, she should pick Faiz in view of the fact that he had the galls to confess his feelings on time. They had had enormous and cavernous memories and attachments. Though Faiz goofed it up, he was always by her side and he wasn't. Faiz also came back to make up for everything later. These things really matter in life, he reckoned. He was obviously not aware of all the troubles and tortures she'd been through, and his pre-conceived notion about her ex was coming from there, she knew. She not only entreated to stop comparing himself with her ex but also revealed the truth about their relationship. "We both had flaws and differences, more than you can assume; differences just as the chasmic gap between a reader and writer. Our relationship sustained only because of my tolerating nature," she expressed. There was a bone of contention; she wanted to be left alone and he wasn't letting it happen. He wanted to call her again and she refused in a huff. He wondered if he had touched the wrong chord, then side-tracked her sullen mood with silly questions about what she was planning to give his daughter, when she would send it and things like that. But nothing was able to stop her from talking about her ex in detail now.

She was able to make out his trick yet preferred to answer only those particular questions in a few words so that he didn't feel disdained. Then, he asked what kind of a man she'd prefer to marry. She dodged his question this time and asked him why he wanted to know. He was wondering what her fans would think when she became popular, when somehow they would alight upon him. They would think he was a jackass for having missed the golden chance of dating her, he expressed. She adduced that Faiz had possessed some of the qualities, like he handled anything with ease and always smelled good. This meant that even if they were dating, she would have kicked him out as he was not very organized though he created less of a mess, he construed.

He also wanted to know why she was not in touch with Faiz now, to which she had an instant reply that she was the one who told him to get married to someone else. They had chosen their separate lives. So, in that way he was also married and had children too, he replied. They had emotional strings attached because of their physical relationship, she responded back. Those were mere biological needs, even he enjoyed sex with his wife, he retorted. She answered retaliating that they had connected beyond the needs that he was referring to. Faiz was her ex-boyfriend whereas he was her friend. **He wrote countering her statement that they were never friends from the start. To that she asked what they were. They were two incomplete stories waiting to be completed, he replied.** Though friendship existed in their relationship, they never saw each other just as friends in real life. She couldn't take the way he undervalued himself in front of her ex and that's why she was defending him from the beginning, he asserted. She always believed that they were good friends and that had kept the flame of their relationship burning. He was right that she was going to choose him even if she had to adjust this way her whole life. They may never get physical or possibly meet but that cannot change her love for him. She just wanted to stay connected with him till her last breaths.

Her love for him had no boundaries or rules. She felt that strongly for him. That day she had realized that Faiz had only come to fill the void after he left without saying anything when she was in the middle of her 2nd year. Her relationship with Faiz was possible because they could see each other. She had always placed Faiz on top of him before this. In fact, she had said all sorts of things to make him feel less important before. Faiz could be irreplaceable, but she can't in all eternity have this kind of a relationship with anyone else again in this birth. He was that 12th of never in her life, she sadly expressed. Her **only confession** had led his value and worth to shine out as gold. Now, she also wanted to drape off the curtains from the past and tell him how she chose to remain with Faiz despite tolerating gruesome behaviour without any fear of judgement. He had feelings for another woman even after marriage so he was in no position of judging her, he responded. Then she gave away the information of her abortions. She was that fool who was stubbornly inflexible, she phrased. She explained how she had spent all the money she had saved in those days on consulting doctors, visiting for scanning, all alone. It so happened that on one of her birthdays, they spent the entire day looking for a clinic away from her work place that would allow a secret abortion. That was the only time when Faiz was with her, all the other times he was concerned that his relatives would spot him with her near the clinic. Only she had to bear the brunt in their relationship, she expressed.

How could she have eaten the vomit again and how could he have the effrontery to leave her after such a catastrophe? How could he drop their children? How could he not marry her? He questioned back, disgruntled and aghast. This was their joint decision, she stressed. They were not prepared for the blaze. They were both students the 1st time she was pregnant, and the 2nd time when it happened, their careers had just begun. Their relationship was on the rocks for different reasons; they could split but she never turned hostile on him, neither took anything to heart. Her attitude changed towards him only after he dumped her, she elucidated. Dheeraj stated that this was precisely the reason he was still with his wife. Both of his children were born unplanned, in fact, he was on a break from his job when the 1st child was born. He obtained his bachelor degree only after his 2nd child. He couldn't pluck up the courage to let on his feelings on time he agreed, but he would never leave his girlfriend in a lurch at such a stage. He was far more responsible and nowhere like him, he retorted.

Until then, he had thought that Faiz must have been someone great, whom she chose over him. She thought he must have hated her equally. If his feelings had turned animus, he could tell her without hesitation, she woefully appealed. He evinced that to him, this was just the foolish version of her, nothing except that had changed for him. In fact, he felt even guiltier because all this mess wouldn't have occurred if he had expressed his feelings on time. He was indirectly responsible for her agony. It was nearly

10 in the morning and her eyes were swollen. Tears were still rolling because he had taken her down to that painful memory lane. He left her to sleep at least 40 winks as he couldn't see her suffer anymore, he said. He had an awful lot of work to do, start unpacking stuff and sort things before immigration, so he left her to repose. She didn't hear a word from him after that. She was plagued by the previous day's emotional turmoil, still waiting for his message eagerly. She knew this day would come when she would part from him and was thinking about it at night when he dropped her back his worries.

Talking about his wife screwed her mind, and she was done with his tautness whenever Silvi created a fuss for him. At the same time, he was distraught with the things going on. "I have no idea how long it will take to get another job in this critical period of corona when I have my family to look after. My relationship with my spouse is only getting worse and I am done compromising and conciliating. Our complicated relationship is stirring my mind and I don't want to live without talking to you regularly. This immense uncertainty is giving me a hard time, the worst is not knowing what is lying ahead," he groaned. He expected her to soften up whenever he was perturbed, but she did the exact opposite this time and simply quoted, "Mysteries and uncertainties are the energies of life, so don't let them scare you unduly." What more could she say when she was herself upset. He had thought that after a tough day he could lean on her, instead she told him not to bother about her anymore and that bit his head even more. Soon he feigned his anger and retorted, "Fine, I won't talk to you." This made her elaborate on her point and she said that it was just a matter of time, everything would be alright. Security was something insipid, so in place of brooding over problems, he would have to put his toe out and wrestle to cut his losses with his wife. His children were in lower grades, so he could take care of them even with his savings until he got a job.

His anger melted at the speed of an ice-cream. As the saying goes, "Lover's anger is short-lived," and there she was, back as his guiding light. Then he knocked in with his ideas as quickly as it took to blink. He said, "I somehow need to find an Indian sim card so that we can pleasantly talk even when I reach India."This was a piece of resolution she cared less about. To her, those were their last moments, and she'd rather think practically and keep his ideas aside. She was prepared to keep him away. His mind was full of blunders, and she didn't want to be an albatross around his neck; he must focus on sorting his life and settle in peace, she propounded.

He also wanted her to make plans to meet, which could be executed successfully. He thought that if he did, he would surely get caught again. His desires were getting deeper and she no longer wanted to entertain this, so she explained what she had slept on for longer. "I am not going to take the blame by planning our meeting. In fact, if you want to meet me, then you would have to plan it with your wife's knowledge. By talking to me secretly, you are only inculcating a doubt that we are having an affair. You are misleading your wife; I don't even like the way you make me switch the app in between our conversations. I feel as if I am your cry pillow. I have cooperated enough to save you from your wife's inquiry. I can't put myself down anymore, it's time you stand up for me." She gave as good as he got this time.

"In this case, our meeting is never going to be possible in this birth. Silvi will not attempt to understand our relationship because she has misunderstandings fed from before, and maybe you haven't noticed that I am messaging you on WA even now. If I had cared to play so safe, then I would have been texting you on telegram all the time. I am waiting to get a new sim card so that I can contact you even after my quarantine period. It has been 14 years we have not seen each other, and I can't wait to see you," he evinced. He would get busy with his family right after quarantine and may not even miss her often. She would lose the importance she had today, she propounded, but he hated it when she decided his mind and put words into his mouth. She wanted to see him herself but didn't want to let any of this emotion get into his head. She was restraining herself for a long time, when deep down even she was as wishful as him.

It was hard for logic to prevail over emotions, so she surrendered by letting her inner desires out. She agreed to meet him but refused to be the schemer. They were canoodling and romancing as if lovers were meeting after a great struggle. Though she craved for his actual indulgence, they could only satiate themselves that way over messages. Like love begets love, this time she wasn't only receiving but returning his intimate hugs and kisses through GIFs. He was the pursuer and she was the pursued, in this case. He was in a state of delirious happiness. Soon it strung her mind and she put to confer – suppose he was happily married; he wouldn't have missed her this madly, isn't it? She was saying whatever occurred to her that night. He could have possibly missed her a little less in that case, however, she would always linger in his mind. He loved her unconditionally and no one could take that place, he answered. After 10 years, she had returned to him what he was longing to hear. She was slightly disconcerted,wondering if she would ever get the chance of expressing her buried love again. Even the next morning, she was talking to him until he got into the queue. She was behaving really loquacious, berating him for not having his breakfast, for not carrying a power bank, for being that ill-equipped, and asking him to keep himself hydrated throughout his travel. For her, that was the only time when she could shower her love, care and attention before he got back to his family. He was sleepy and inactive, so he responded a little nettled. His concern between all her tiny gabby was still whether he would be able to arrange for another sim card so that he could talk to her on call instead of chatting all the time. It would also save him from Silvi's investigations and atrocities.

She would also prefer speaking on a call and that was just for his satisfaction, she baited.

The next afternoon, her phone was flooded with pictures of the deluxe room he was staying in, the morning meal he ate, his bed, and a mobile number written on a piece of paper. Like they say, "Fathers and sons are more considerate of one another than mothers and daughters, there is no love greater than a father to his son." It was his father who had surprised him by handing him an Indian sim card along with the eatables that same morning. She was surprised too, but how thoughtful of him, she enthused. He had an inexplicable connection with his father, not only of flesh and blood, but their hearts were accountable too, he gleefully expressed. That gesture had helped him attain a coup but she was not at rest. Little did his father know that this help could turn out to be a cause of disaster at some point. Unlimited free calls and net packs were going to make a seismic change in their lives. This portion of life was a twist of fate. He called the same night, as she was still stuck with her promise of not initiating a call that she had taken years back when he had lied to her about having a girlfriend. He started spieling about his traumatizing experience from the airport till he was accommodated in one of the 3-star hotels in Patthantada. He seemed to have found their service pretty lousy, it didn't come close to any of his expectations. He was whining about the mosquitoes; he was unhappy about many things except that he could talk to her about it all.

She insisted he ask his father to fetch a mosquito repellent but for some reason he didn't want to bother him. She didn't find it appropriate to interfere in his private matter as to why he had developed such an attitude towards him unless he shared on his own, so she started another topic. She could talk about his appetencies and fervours. He felt that she could really start the conversation but to her, he had the gift of the gab. It was true that once they got engaged in their conversations, it became hard for them to disconnect the call unless his balance itself got over, which was not going to be the case here. They would have to take a call of hanging up on their own. They must have said good night at least 6 times, which made him arrive at a decision that he would not call her everyday. If he continuously received what he derives great pleasure from, he'll become addicted, he spoke. On the contrary, she had an ardent impulse to live in the present rather than dwell on the clouds of anticipation. She didn't want to think about what was coming up tomorrow that she hadn't seen yet, she wanted to live every moment that she had with him undaunted.

She rightly quoted, "No amount of **regretting** can change the past, no amount of worrying can change the future. Nobody can peep into the age-old illusion of tomorrow. Tomorrow is tomorrow, future cares have future cures. So, we must mind our today. Who knows, God may add tomorrow to the present hour." She knew she may not get more time with him as she did in those days. What she equally worried about, was that in the coming days, they may not be able to contact each other for many reasons and their days together, whichever way she considered, were numbered. She had no time to lose; because she knew nothing with certainty. However, she let him take his call. When the mind is in a state of uncertainty, the smallest impulse directs it to either side, so he didn't resist talking to her everyday.

He checked her availability by leaving her messages at first, whereas she had already given him the liberty of calling her whenever he wanted to talk. She didn't string politeness by such things but wanted to make him feel loved, she explained. They began to run on a set pattern and the result was remaining to be seen, especially with him, as he was not allowed to step out of the hotel till his test results came negative. He was bound to co-operate with the practices of the hotel that made him do things at particular times. He would channel all his energy in doing activities that he loved during the day and at night, they would speak. There was no source of interruption and he didn't have to dislodge any activities. Healthy eating and physical exertion were his proclivity. The room had a TV if he simply wanted to get hooked or entertained. He could talk to his children any length of time he wanted to. Everything was happening in due course. This must have been the best time of his life, his best career break.

A week later, he was taken for a Covid test, and they were talking till he walked to the ambulance. He realized his relationship with her was going deeper and he couldn't breathe peacefully without thinking of her. What he feared was happening; he was going to be out in a few days, back to his house in Kerala with his family. He was dreading his release because it would keep her away. His illusionary fears were getting him flustered and he was diffusing into a mild state of anxiety. She tried to cool him by assuring him that she was there for him, to assuage his fear, to nib his bud at the moment, to prepare him for the fall. She was on the same footing but held herself strong before the man who she had first gifted things to. To the man she had feelings for from the time she knew nothing much about this world.

That night, her soul became more alive and she expressed her wish to die in his arms on her last day on this earth. He said he couldn't promise to appear at that juncture where he'd lose her forever. He was subjected to a similar experience earlier when his mother was afflicted with jaundice, post her cancer cure. His mother was suffering the death of a thousand cuts and he was the only one with her when her health deteriorated all of a sudden. She would have foreseen herself standing at death's door. She somehow mumbled one thing on his ear and that was to take care of his brothers. She had fallen next to him in the ambulance when their hands were still clenched together. She was cold halfway to the hospital; he could feel it but wasn't willing to accept the truth. Bhaiya was studying Engineering at that time, so he had to complete all the rituals on his behalf, but be that as it may, bhaiya was the one closer to their mother. He was the apple of her eye. After completing the rituals, he locked himself in the bathroom, which was outside the house as normally found in every house of Kerala, and bellowed in mental anguish. He had held his tears for really long in spite of being devastated, he spieled.

He brought up the talk of these incidents to prove to her that he was not 'fattu' like she had perceived in their School days. He also wanted to clear her perception of him being 'kanjus' from those days. In an attempt, he explained that whenever his mother was taken out for treatment, he used to be left alone to take care of his brothers that's why he was asked to handle the money matters in the house. He had a wallet with a tidy sum of pocket money, which is why most of his batchmates were in his company. He would still spend money at a drop of a dime whenever they pushed him to buy eatables. He used to do all the household chores and then come to class, but sometimes would miss having his breakfast. He would walk into the canteen with a ravenous appetite in the morning, and being followed at such times by his batchmates was what he used to find the real heights of shamelessness. "Earlier, I had assumed that being a Malayali South Indian, you would possess cupidity, so I named you 'kanjus'. I thought of you as a coward, clearly based on our story. The other remarks were consciously made," she replied.

One day, he had asked her to remind him to tell her why his relationship with his father had changed, but she was desolated into a pensive mood. He was going to vacate the hotel and she was thinking all about their complicated relationship. But before he left, she wanted him to answer what she meant to him. She was his lantern in the darkness, she was irreplaceable, he answered, but now these answers weren't enough. She dug deeper and asked him right away if he could marry her. "I wouldn't want you to marry a divorcee. Secondly, my children need their mother, so I can't let them suffer. I can go to any extent, even turn any less unscrupulous to meet their needs. I may not have been good in other relations, but I at least want to be the best father to them. My wife is my cross to bear now, so I can't just break all ties with her. You may not need me in every phase of life, but I need you, so your presence itself is valuable," he explained.

This pinned down her limited importance because where men consider needs, women consider wants. She wisely replied that he couldn't sail on two boats and the message was clear for him. He was going to leave her life at that very moment. She was grief-stricken yet projected a brave heart. "Women are only made to look complicated by a man who isn't man enough when he can't provide the things she deserves," she cried. Afterwards, she left a one-word answer in the message, LEAVE!

She was glum for a few days, and there he was unsettled and wretched. No amount of love showered could convince her now, so he left a note for her to read. He had always seen her being convivial but he was facing her now. Even after reading his love-filled messages, she was like a buckskin and he was trying every trick to get her to interact with him again. Lastly, he shrieked and wrote, "How cold blooded and stone hearted you've become, my love. How earnestly I wanted to share my father's matter but it looks like I will die carrying even this bitter part of my life." His attempt to induce some soft emotion in her worked and she called him right back. Her silence had been killing him for the last 3 days, and when he finally heard her voice, he was reduced to tears. He was trying to take control of his quavering voice when she said she would hear him out regarding his father, and once he reached his house, it was all over between them. She said all this without being infuriated, which surprised him. This wasn't a call for truce, this was her way of saying goodbye, he understood.

A lover's anger is fuel to love, they say. For him, just the thought of having her away was scary, he'd prefer to die without her, and here she had decided to leave him forever, he sadly replied. She could somehow convert his lost interest in vouchsafing about his changed relationship with his father. It took him a while to sort of digest the fact, then he began to articulate thinking that this may be their last moment together before he left for home. He said he was the one who had convinced his father for a 2nd marriage, so that his father was not left alone after his mother passed away. It had even cost him a slap on his cheek the 1st time he proposed this idea. The only thing they knew about his 2nd mother from her background verification before the wedding was that she was a widow with a son. Later, they found out that her husband had committed suicide by burning himself, which they didn't consider a big deal. But soon after their marriage, they observed some behavioural anomalies and unsoundness of mind in her. However, before they could unravel anything, she sneaked off one night. They couldn't find her, but she hadn't stolen anything from home while leaving. He had nothing to do with his father's 3rd marriage; his father was solely involved in finding his 3rd mother from a matrimonial site. However, he couldn't get along with her due to her prodigality and issues of improvidence. She frittered away on picking expensive things, and once even raised concerns about property in front of everyone, asking who would take care of her welfare, what was her share going to be after his father's death, and so on. He doubted that she was the one to put a bug in his father's ears against him, and since he didn't want to spell trouble for his father, he never demanded anything. All she could advise was not to put the cart before the horse and work on making their relationship better before everything got worse.

His most awaited day arrived; he was released from the hotel, which was no less than 14 days of exile, physically cutting off from the world. He was left to experience the remaining 14 days of quarantine in the comfort of his own house. In the morning, he evinced that he would surely meet her at least once before they grew old, at least once in his lifetime. Life was unpredictable and she may not be alive till he was ready, so if they couldn't meet any day then it was their loss together, not hers or his alone. And that's why she wasn't lying in any wait, is what she put across as a hint that she didn't expect or trust him now.

He pinged her again in a few days, stating that he was really thankful to her for being his wingman, being kind towards him, and considering him. He wanted to lend her his help as a means of repayment, so he asked if he could be useful in any manner. He just wanted to let her know that he was available despite realizing how self-sufficient and independent she was. "The only way to help me would be helping yourself," she retorted. He was just looking for ways to connect with her again, whereas she was trying to avoid him as far as possible to save herself from more hurt. Their cravings for a private conclave were escalating, making them impatient. There was a burning desire in them to express their love physically, which she, having already hung in vast disappointment, obviously wouldn't have let out.

So, he dropped her a text stating that he was coming to meet her or he could arrange their meeting in Kerala so that he got to show his house as well. She could pick whichever plan suited her best, he exclaimed. He also sent her pictures of his house. He lived on the outskirts of

Pattantada and his house lurked between the dense forests. He was taking photographs of the whole place as they both were ardent lovers of nature and its aesthete. What got her respond instantly were the pictures of peacocks dancing in his garden. He was ravished by this glorious morning and homecoming, and the only thing missing to him now was her picture. He was expecting a normal picture of her, of how she looked when she woke up. But the midclose-up selfie had her wearing just a spaghetti top, which greatly appealed to him. He developed an erotic mood and they were slowly getting frenzy. Their hearts were set on those carnal instincts but he had never experienced sex chat before. His wife was the only lady he had got intimate with. There were no surprises or passion in their love making. They enjoyed routine foreplay before the actual intercourse, whenever their biological clocks ticked. It had never started with hugs and kisses; he didn't even remember if she had ever hugged him. But all that was nothing compared to the level of satisfaction he got merely from their conversation. He just knew that after making love with her, he wouldn't be able to lie with his wife again. From the time their relation had grown to this state of expressing carnal feelings, he found even all love emojis that his wife sent to him pretty faded. He would be supremely attached, if they ever got physical, he expressed.

There was a wave of satyriasis passing through them already and her selfie added fuel to it. He explained how he would establish a sensual love making scene with her.

First, he was going to hug her tight, then carry her in his arms and make her lie on the bed. In fact, she would nicely fit into his arms. He was equally going to seize the opportunity to live his concupiscence. Before he undressed her, he would kiss her on the lips and all over that face he had waited to see and touch. Then, as he undressed her, he would indulge her in foreplay. He would move his covetous hands all over her body, caressing, kissing, and licking. He would then let her straddle on him. After getting enough nooky, when they reached the point of bonking, they would lock themselves in their favourable position and hit it hard and fast. As he found the pre and post coitus acts more interesting, he would want to remain in that erogenous zone and let the pleasure go on. He knew that women intensely desired bonding, so he would spoon her, wrap her in his arms, and watch her after everything.

He would also love to be nestled in her arms, engaged in her invigorating touch. He would stroke her body with his fingertips, interlock their hands and kiss them. He would feed her need for intimacy even if his orgasms were dazed. They could talk or silently enjoy the shagged up. Because men love to hear about their sizzling sex skills, her feedback would stay in his mind for a long time. For him, this was going to be a nice booty wrap, but for her, she'd prefer to snuggle up under the shower to shut down his snooze reflex and electrify his body. This would keep their blood flow stimulated, energize their bodies rather than having them drained quickly in bed. They could later settle down to cuddling in bed and dozing off after sweet exhaustion from sex, she added. He had swept her off his feet by talking all frisky; he was aroused and she was wet by the end of their sex chats.

In the next few days, he bought a bullet and happened to accomplish one of his other wishes from the bucket list. Now, he was claiming that he could come to meet her in full throttle at her place in Bangalore if she was not willing to come to Kerala. He could just come any day and take her by surprise. He would clear the deck without having her to worry even a little, he propounded. He was toing and froing about it in excitement, and had taken her GPS location because his home quarantine period was finally getting over. Their relationship had changed from the time of lockdown and he was afraid she would be crushed and consumed after he left. If she could promise that their relationship wouldn't change and that she would cope with the setbacks or that she wouldn't fall prey to depression, only then would they seclude themselves in the hotel room, he proposed. His desires were not as important as her peace of mind. He didn't want her to remember him as one treacherous adulterer. Then, there wouldn't be any difference between him and her ex. He was happy just with their casual meeting outside and would be immensely pleased to see her after a long wait. To him, that was primary, he explained.

After her harrowing experience in the past, she was afraid to think of anything worse happening to her, but still she gave him the permission to come uninformed. She wanted things to unwind by themselves in front of her. Later one day, his wife created chaos because she had a hunch that he was having an affair with someone, and her prime suspect was Prema. She sledge hammered an argument with him for staying online on WA for a long time. She kept her call in conference with bhaiya and dragged the children into it too this time. What's even egregious was that she was trying to cast unpropitious behaviour in their children towards him. She insisted that their 2nd son question him about having an illicit affair with another woman. At the same time, Silvi nagged him to tow her as well over the call for clarity between the truth and a lie. Bhaiya mollified the situation and somehow quietened her, but he seemed askance at Silvi's truculent behaviour.

Bhaiya came to understand that it could be only Prema that his wife was talking about, but without drawing any conclusions, he preferred to ask Dheeraj what the matter actually was. When he explained everything, right from how he had met his wife to how things were going between them even after marriage, bhaiya spoke forthright that he had written his fate worse than death by marrying her. He would have to compromise and face his wife for the sake of their children now. He still couldn't come out clean when bhaiya asked why he didn't confront such contentious issues before. His wife stayed with her own parents on numerous occasions when he was working in Kerala. When he sent her and the children back to

India from Dubai because he had vacated the flat during their migration, her parent's house was her easy residence. That's how his wife and children's stay became consistent there. His younger brother, Surya had once witnessed them having a huge fight during his visit to her parent's house. After which, he had mentioned to Dheeraj that being the most charming and intelligent among the brothers, he could have easily spotted someone more educated and beautiful. He had on his own favoured her and took chances on her, that's why he always masked his marital issues by smiling, he expressed. Even his other younger brother, Prakash had earlier relayed about his wife to bhaiya, so it wasn't hard to believe that Silvi could hype the matter even if they spoke only as friends.

By this time, bhaiya had discerned that they were in touch, but couldn't make out if they were really having an affair. This whole incident would have anyway pinched him that something was kept secret. He reckoned that it would be wise not to involve her by raising concerns without any evidence, she could happen to insult them instead. Also, he must stop being dead honest to his wife because she doesn't seem to deserve it. In a state of scepticism, bhaiya said that he could turn to him anytime for help. Complete mayhem broke out in his family until the next day when it reached his father's ears. His father took charge and ruled the roost without discussing anything with Dheeraj. His father was one of those that Silvi was highly alarmed of, so when his father called her up and instructed that she should start living with her husband right after quarantine at their house in Pattantada, she had no other choice but to obey him. He was frightened when his wife put them all on a conference call; he was in trepidation until bhaiya called him in the evening. To both of them, the circumstances were so stormy that they ended conversing over WA since that day.

It was after this day that she believed about their shotgun situational marriage and purposely asked him to expatiate about his wife and how they got married all over again. It gave her some glimmer behind his wife's suspicious character and she ascribed that Silvi's insecurities were from her own over-indulgence on the phone with that pen friend cum boyfriend with whom she was about to elope. As he was often online or on call, she interpreted that as an affair. She understood that he had a soft spot for women in his heart and couldn't see any woman suffer. However, the ugly truth was that he hadn't saved her from committing suicide that evening but had dug his own grave. He felt meek on her emotional coercion and stooped impulsively, otherwise there was no need for him to be threatened. He wouldn't have been trapped even if that affair stormed into a police case. She would have been proven guilty on further investigation. She was vulnerable, accepted, but he could have handled the situation differently. He had taken a lifetime's decision in a snap without knowing her well. He didn't have to take the bait of marrying her. He shouldn't have pledged for something he wasn't sure of. On top of that, he had misled her by hiding her in his flat for 7 days instead of taking her back to her family the very next day. Even after all this, if he had quit while he was ahead, he could have saved his day.

When she imparted these thoughts on him, he started worrying about how he would face his wife now that he was indeed having an affair with the same person she constantly doubted. He couldn't claim that he was not in love, and if he came clean, she wouldn't spare him for sure. She would go to the bitter end to hurt him. Not only would she turn their children against him, he would equally lose every chance of taking action on her. His life would change from bad to worse, he vented.

He was of the type who wouldn't even hurt a flea. His wife was aware of this and that's why she knew when and how to attack, and how to dominate and take control of him. He would have to hold onto this truth, otherwise he would not be able to expose her. There was absolutely no use arguing for the loss toss, so he'd have to be really chary while speaking about anything to Silvi. He could start by disclosing that he was not the one that their daughter was going to elope with. He would need to unfold her doings for her parents, so they learnt about her improprieties, and only then could he take the situation over from her. He wouldn't let her intrude into his privacy without his will and strictly refrain her from touching his phone. Let her experience living with her in-laws and other family members. Let her start working and shouldering half of his responsibilities. Let her step out of that comfort zone and face the world. An empty mind is a devil's workshop, so she'll have no time to think about unnecessary things when she was occupied. He'd have to be austere and teach her discipline, the right and wrong attitude, stop over-bearing and start treating her like an adult.

He would book an appointment with a psychiatrist and behest her that they were heading there without a word of protest. Tell her that he had sought enough permission, and as her husband he had every right to express concern about her mental health and check on his doubts about her. She wouldn't obey him otherwise. He must not come to her terms without thinking on his feet hereon. He could take his worth and grants in life only through these right actions. She could be from any kind of family but that does not stop her from learning and possessing higher virtues. He must not focus only on their children but also on making her strong and independent. Maybe, when he sees things turn the corner, he would fall in love with her. Gradually, his family atmosphere would become healthier and he would be happy. He may then not even feel the necessity of leaking out the news of their affair. He may not hark back at her as often as he does now. In fact, he may not need her anymore, Prema counselled.

For now, he had to understand that he couldn't just rip the band aid off and try to get rid of this problem. He had to keep the faith, she pointed out, trying to assuage his tension. Just a few days after that bummer, Prema put forward to him her proposal of marriage again. Like they say, "All is fair in love and war." After some serious thinking, she arrived at this conscious decision that she could walk down the aisle with him in good time. She may need a few years to settle down in her career and then she would be ready to take care of his children. He could even divorce his wife that time, she spoke. He voiced that he couldn't just walk out of this marriage and disarm his wife. His children were his prime asset and that was the only reason he was living with his wife today. He would have left her long ago if they were not there. He still felt that of all the titles he's had the privilege of having, being a dad was the best.

He was also bound by Hindu rituals according to which he was supposed to have only one wife. Besides, he wouldn't be able to give proper time on either side and do justice to any of them. He was not supposed to have an extra-marital affair and what's even sad was that he didn't feel guilty about it, he exculpated. She had every right on him and deserved him more than anyone else. Having said that, he wouldn't be able to take that stand right then even if he wanted to. He had taken the high road for everything except her, he knew that, but he couldn't find a way out of this marriage. She'd have to understand that his hands were tied and he didn't want her lying on any delusive hope, he besieged.

Where there's a will, there's a way. All the good and bad reasons appear when you do or don't want to be with someone, she uttered. She was filled with indignation and desolation for many days. He was trying to talk to her, but she wouldn't respond to any of his messages or calls. His answers were stuck in her mind. On the 4th day, she decided to answer his call to tell him that maybe she's just another woman in his life, like the one on this side. It felt as if she was reaching for the moon if she thought that he'd ever marry her in this birth. She cried like a baby and called herself a 'dasi'. The word poked at his heart too and he was breaking down. He wanted to disconnect the call and cry out loud, but she didn't even let him do that. She was trying to elicit why he didn't revert to her whenever she said, "I LOVE YOU!" before their calls ends. She had always loved him but he didn't seem to respect any of her feelings and emotions. No! No! No! However silly he may have been, he had also loved her from the time she had not even seen him, and not in his wildest dreams could he think of her as a 'dasi', he confessed. He appeared rough and tough in his exterior, so she could never imagine him bursting out like that. However, her grief and anger were ruling that moment. "You call and message me as and when you feel like. You choose to appear and disappear at your own intervals. You at times distance yourself and at times pull me close. You may not have realized but your actions don't complement your thoughts," she uttered.

She left him in the same state of befuddlement. The next day, he was raising concern for his feeling of depression. "I am getting close to feeling of ending my life. I think I am the culprit and the root cause of everyone's destruction – your, my father and my own wife. I deserve to die; nature would take its course after my demise, and Silvi will take care of our children somehow," he wrote. He was the one who broke the news of Sushant Singh Rajput's suicide the same morning. The moment she went through that news forward and read his messages, she warned him not to take any drastic steps before talking to her, otherwise she would never forgive him. She called early that night and tried to make him feel at ease by expressing her understanding of his situation. He was no coward to run away from his responsibilities. "Life's never easy for anyone," she stated. He wanted to get wise up if he had been selfish with her as he always had the impression that he was selfless towards her. How could he hurt her so much when he loved her so much? If he respected women, then he wouldn't have slapped his wife. He was aware that he'd been unfair on many occasions but never knew that he had treated her that insensitively. Did she feel disillusioned of him as a good human now? He questioned.

She was someone he liked to turn to for everything in life. He was the happiest in her company, even if she was the cause of his bane too. So he accepted to be selfish to fulfil his need to be with her. But there were times when he was equally selfless. Back in 2011, when he had messaged her with an intention to propose, she had just stepped into a relationship with her ex. Their religion was the cause of conflict, so if he had attempted to open up, there were chances he could easily conquer her, instead he chose to back out. That relatively proved his selflessness, she averred. In relation to his wife, he would have to accept that she was least bothered about him. She cared for a secure future and family, which he provided without having to make any effort, unlike her. She was a blessed woman, whether in terms of a husband, family or children, which she didn't want to recognize. Love was not so important for her; though she used her children as a weapon for emotional threat, she would never have the courage of divorcing him.

She'd taken him for granted since he had enormous patience and had never turned hostile on her. She knew how to seek forgiveness from him. She knew he would go easy on her once she apologized. She was someone impenitent and that's why she kept on disrespecting him from the start. She threw her doubtful arrows and he fell into the trap. Even if her accusations weren't true, she still felt like she had nothing to lose unless someday he only left her. Either he would get caught or she would grab a fat chance of arguing, the art of which was instilled in her by default. While this was a win-win situation for her, it disrupted his state of normalcy. Some people got entertained by another's destruction. Perhaps she was one of them. She did not cease her wickedness even after getting a slap for accusing him of sleeping with his own mother. That's why it was not his fault, even then she would suggest not to raise his hands on her again. She was the mother of 3 children now and in order to correct her, he had to practice good behaviour. Enough of talking hem and haw, he needed to change his on-going soft attitude first and plot efficacious plans in his head for a quicksilver change in his life, she counselled. He shouldn't let the grass grow more under his feet and remember that there's always light at the end of the tunnel, all his efforts would feel worthy in the end, she phrased.

The more she dredged up about her, the more she found her repellent, but she had to guide him to help him ride out to the point of extrication. However, she hung onto massive discontentment from the day he rejected her proposal for the 2nd time. He was talking about how he would slink when no one was around and show her his baby girl over a video call some day after his release. But she was lost, floundering on whether or not she should see him in the first place. The moment he finished, she went off tangent and intonated that she was not sure if she wanted to see him. She needed to prepare her mind to face him after that hard decision made on her, she replied in utter disconsolate. It was a little imperceptible the way she derailed his idea. Without catechizing further, he said that it was okay and he wouldn't force her. She must have thought about it prior to leading to this decision. To him, it appeared as if she had made up her mind long ago. He would wait until she was ready, he exclaimed. She made a beautiful video on account of Father's Day, showcasing his pictures with only his children this time. She also created an attractive blog page to display all his art. She documented some of his beautiful sketches to itemize his journey of quarantine from the airport to the hotel in a video format. He had drawn them during his stay in the hotel with an idea of using these frames to report his story, and that's when it hit her that she could make them more creative. She let him do the script and voice-over as well. She recorded in her own voice and dedicated the same song, 'PehlaNasha', which he used to repeatedly listen to on his walkman in their School days. She chipped in by forwarding his resume and cover letter wherever she could to serve her network for his purpose.

He felt indebted for all the things she had done for him, so he was looking for ways to express his gratitude. He knew she liked western wear and sent her links to some shopping sites to let her check out the kind of clothes she would like. He wanted to buy them for her. She may not like the idea of him transferring money to her account, he was aware, but in these hard times, he felt he should at least attempt to lend her fiscal help and spoke about it with great courage over a message. He was overwhelmed and speechless after watching the Father's Day video. However, he raised a small nugatory concern the moment they came on call. He was worried that his wife would begin to grill him on the images of flowers that belonged to her garden, which were used to relate to his children. Nowadays, one could pull out any damn thing from the internet and edit however they wanted. He could easily convince his wife by simply saying that his friend had made the video. He decided it was better to not let her watch as he feared her investigation. He was behaving quite preposterously, overstating his concern and that got to her nerves. Not only did she hung up on him, but it was the shortest they had spoken that night. She hadn't expected such an untoward outcome of absurdity. His reasons were pretty inane and that left her feeling below par. She ended up not speaking to him for 2 long days.

Her anger stayed overnight and began diffusing in the morning, but she needed time to prepare her mind to have him gone in just a couple of days after his quarantine. She was mourning his loss in his presence. She was slow on her uptake to understand that their love was liberated and immortal. It isn't wrong to expect something as a lover, but love didn't always entail marriage. From his end, marriage was not going to be possible, so she was willing to take his abstinence and leave him forever if it was for his good. She just wanted to meet him once before she parted ways with him and so she took the call of meeting him in Kerala. She asked him to book tickets once the bus services resumed and covid settled down for safe travel. At the same time, she would hand him gifts for his daughter. She had set her sight on it now, she declared.

He was chuffed to bits because she had floated his boat with this decision. He started divulging his plans, forwarded lists of places that had facilities of house boating at a good price. They would ride on his new bullet, pass through places familiar for site-seeing on their way and check into a nice hotel once she arrived, he expressed with glee. He had enthusiastically set out everything in his head and she was equally delighted. But she also wanted him to seek God's blessings before he started his new life after heading back to his little family. Therefore, she insisted he go on a ride alone and pamper himself a bit, spend some time with himself and nature now that he was finally going to be able to explore the world outside again. The day he was released, he checked in for a morning relaxing session where he got his hair and beard done. Then he headed off somewhere, she didn't intrude. It was the temple of Lord Ram at the cliff, which was established long after the history where once one side of Jatayu's wing had fallen at that place after Ravan had clipped off. The incident had occurred when Jatayu was trying to save Sita after he spotted her in a flying chariot while Ravan was kidnapping her. He would still send her pictures, updating her on what he was up to even when she had clearly refrained from contacting her the day before. One of the pictures that she received in the late evening indicated that he was boozing with a few of his close paternal relatives.

He was highly inebriated when he called her that night and that too for sometime. It was only him talking about how much he loved her over and over again. How he couldn't think of himself being separated from her. He was already woozy and before he stomped off, he wanted to make himself heard loud and clear. He was totally hammered with the same gang for 3 consecutive days. The next day was a bit different as he spoke confidently and not in haste. He had visited another temple the next morning, one just beside his house. Our ancestors believed that one could supplicate but in return needed to deliver what one had pledged for after all their 3 wishes were accomplished. He spoke about making one of the wishes in her favour, so that it could help her fulfil her plans. She was impressed with him for being that thoughtful and found him decent enough to ask if she kept the standard of not entertaining any drunken man because his wife didn't seem to like it herself. Silvi felt offended by his approach at such times. So, he apologized for the previous day as well, if she had felt the same way.

He had gathered with his relatives like that just, getting blitzed and gabbing after really long, otherwise he drank only occasionally after rehab. He had headed that kind of meeting off at the pass, he mentioned. His joys were emanated though his slurred speech didn't fail to reflect his blithe. When the next person is not in the same consciousness as hers, she listened without talking much. Therefore, she replied that no, she didn't have any issues unless he started misbehaving. After he was grogged, he wouldn't remember any part of it the next day, she knew. It was true that a drunken man's words couldn't be completely trusted, but their mind spoke the most sober heart. So, on the 3rd day, he asked her to double check and confirm everything that he had said earlier that she felt doubtful or was half-minded about. For her, this was a golden chance to check his integrity and truthfulness, and she put to question what bothered her the most. Had he really wished that she developed feelings for him when they were in School? Had people in his College recognized her as his girlfriend? Had he really messaged her with the intention of proposing when she was in her 3rd year? Had he ever thought of marrying her or was it only a relationship he was looking for?

She had heard everything he was going to say before except for some additional facts. Back when he was a drug fiend, those pipe dreams lent him immense pleasure because he couldn't have her around. So it was in his figment of imagination that she had brought food and was taking care of his mother when she was sick and hospitalized. The girls in his College had seen him avoiding woeful attention and heard many times that he had been rejecting proposals. Hence, it wasn't hard to convince his batchmates that he was committed. But once he spoke a little loud and spilled his guts to everyone in his class that he was committed to a lady named Prema and was going to marry her in the near future. He counted on his prayers that she developed feelings for him much before she had noticed him in School. He used to accompany Madhavan to the temple sometimes, but once he came inside and knelt before our deities and prayed that if he could have his mother and her forever. Unfortunately, he lost both one after another after that day. He had been afraid to ask for anything ever since. Many years later, just because she expressed this wish, he visited the temple and prostrated himself before God again.

No one can miss the thorns while journeying through the flowery garden of their lives. Similarly, he had been beaten by the ugly stick in his marriage, which had led him to an awful doom, he agreed. He deserved to be oppressively punished for not being able to give her the right and position she truly deserved. He swore on her that if life ever gave him another chance of redoing the espousal, he'd approach her, get down on his knees no matter where she was, if she was still single at that time. He couldn't miss her again; he would like to at least give it a try. He would be the happiest person if she was his partner, he expressed.

They only had a day left before he was going to his wife's place to pick her and the children. She was weeping quietly here while he was speaking over there. Later, she began to snivel such that she choked and quaked, unable to say anything. They were sailing together in this misfortune. They had nothing more than **regrets** at that stage of their lives. That time, he was playing with a strong mind and was being inexorable. He was trying to calm her down and passing kisses on the phone to comfort her. That night, he happened to spell out that he loved her so many times. Their relation was honing to a great depth, they had that love that said, **love to death**. He was a good whistler and she could only get him to do it on her demand. He started whistling 'Pehla Nasha' to make her smile.

The next day, before he went on to continue the same episode of boozing, she interrupted him by saying that this much intoxication would hamper his body, and that she couldn't allow him to drink under her knowledge anymore. He wanted to enjoy life on his own terms and feel liberated one last day before he went back to living a monotonous and disgusting one with his wife. It was only his children who were drawing him back there, not his wife, he coughed out. However, that night, he was drained out and failed to call her even. Maybe his body couldn't take the alcohol. After he pushed back home that evening, he barfed and rolled to bed.

On their last night, he was walking her through his plans like a helpless person. He would hand his i Phone to his wife and buy a basic cell so that he could contact her every morning during his jogging time. Also, he would inform Silvi that she didn't have the permission to touch his phone henceforth. He would send her the postal address of his office for courier once his job was fixed. He was going to video call her the moment he was alone with his daughter. She was simply nodding her head and saying, "Hmm..." because for her, he was yet to live up to his words. She couldn't really take his words as an assurance as she had had similar experiences with him before. If she believed him for what he just said a few minutes ago, it would be like living in a fool's paradise.

At that stage of his life, his entire happiness rested on fixing issues related to his wife and then his job. So, she wished all the odds to be in his favour, after which he may even stop sparing thoughts about her, but that was fine. As long as he was able to live peacefully, she would have **no regrets** about making that wish. Just like how he could do anything to see that his children were happy, similarly, she could do anything to see him happy too, she expressed. It came to her as if she had been holding a gas balloon for a long time and had to now release it. The further it went, it wouldn't be visible but she knew it would go where it belonged. This was the best way she could commemorate the luminous days of their lives together.

The next afternoon, he was primping to check if he was looking neat. The effort was for some politician that he may possibly encounter on his way. His nephew had arranged a short distance meeting with the MLAs to try his luck at getting contracts. His nephew was helping him make his way. He called her during the pit stop when he was waiting for them. They would have barely spoken for 5 minutes that day and that was it. She didn't know what exactly happened after that with him. But after about 8 months, when she was already settled as a Copywriter in another organization, he became active on social media as well as the group. He had started his own contract company and displayed the logo visible on his profile, she could see. Later, he even shared pictures when half of his dream museum construction was completed. He continued to seek some ways to convey his progress though he never cared to message her personally.

She responded being quite practical in the group by giving thumbs up signs on other School friend's opinions and praises about his work. But the separation was painful for her to bear initially. Though she was prepared for this day, she didn't snap back that easily. She was reading his last conversations saved on telegram, listening to his voice messages over and over again, watching all his romantic GIFs, gawking at his pictures that she had saved from FB every night on bed. She was under a huge effect for at least a week after he left. All kinds of thoughts were running through her mind. She was thinking that maybe he'd been busy hunting for a job. Maybe he'd break the news once things got better. Maybe he was entangled in family affairs. Maybe he was exchanging blows with his wife; any level of disputes with her was enough to make him feel tortured and here he was off on this big mission of transforming her. She assumed all the possibilities to make herself feel less miserable. She was thinking of him every time as if she was tarrying at one place just waiting to hear from him. No matter what she did, those thoughts would hit her back. "His silence depicted total negligence, and I won't accept any excuse, however exultant I appear, when he comeback remembering me. I will teach him a nice lesson that will stay with him forever," she said to herself.

EPILOGUE

She was that sensible woman whose heart was guided when taking him as lover and whose head was guided when wanting to take him as a husband. Month after month ran like clappers, but she still had a 'belief' that someday he would appear in front of her house just like that. She was certain because they hadn't said goodbye to one another yet. Looked like what she foreboded came true, she said after musing about it for some time. But I could clearly see, in that state of devastation, what kept her going was 'hope'. Maybe this universe was against their meeting, but the day they come face to face, I'm sure this earth will show some sign of their inexplicable joy.

I was soaked into feeling disconsolate for a few days after completing this book. I had carried them for 9 months, remembering the highs and lows of their lives every day, going into flashbacks to our days together as well because just like them, we haven't met since School. So, are you now wondering if they will remain just incomplete stories that are waiting to be completed? Will they ever meet? If yes, then where exactly would they meet? And what would happen when they meet? Then perhaps you must put on your headphones and listen to this beautiful song by Whitney Houston, "I will always love you". It wasn't easy for me as a writer to let go of the pain that my best friend had been through. I found the lyrics quite suitable to her situation in which even I was living for as long as it took me to write the ending. And the way it's sung may give you goose bumps and tears, out of what you may be feeling for her, or the song may stay with you for your own personal losses.

Lyrics

If I should stay, I would only be in your way. So, I will go but I know, I will think of you every step of the way.

And I will always love you. Will always love you. You, my darling you.

Bitter, sweet memories that is all I am taking with me, so please don't cry, we both know, I am not what you need.

And I will always love you. I will always love you.

But I hope life treats you kind, and I hope you have all you dreamed of, and I wish you joy and happiness but above all this I wish you love.

And I will always love you. You, darling I love you. I will always, I will always love you.